D0294882

ULLIN MACBETH

Recent Titles by Christine Marion Fraser

The Rhanna Series

RHANNA
RHANNA AT WAR
CHILDREN OF RHANNA
RETURN TO RHANNA
SONG OF RHANNA
STORM OVER RHANNA
STRANGER ON RHANNA
A RHANNA MYSTERY

The King's Series

KING'S CROFT
KING'S ACRE
KING'S EXILE
KING'S EXILE
KING'S FAREWELL

The Noble Series

NOBLE BEGINNINGS
NOBLE DEEDS

ULLIN MACBETH*

* *available from Severn House*

ULLIN MACBETH

Christine Marion Fraser

This first world edition published in Great Britain 1996 by
SEVERN HOUSE PUBLISHERS LTD of
9–15 High Street, Sutton, Surrey SM1 1DF.
First published in the USA 1996 by
SEVERN HOUSE PUBLISHERS INC. of
595 Madison Avenue, New York, NY 10022.

British Library Cataloguing in Publication Data

Fraser, Christine Marion
Ullin MacBeth
1. English fiction – 20th century – Scottish authors
2. Scottish fiction – 20th century
I. Title
823.9′14 [F]

ISBN 0-7278-4976-X

All situations in this publication are fictitious and
any resemblance to living persons is purely coincidental.

Typeset by Palimpsest Book Production Limited,
Polmont, Stirlingshire
Printed and bound in Great Britain by
Hartnolls Ltd, Bodmin, Cornwall.

To Tracy
For whom the Island of Mull holds
many happy childhood memories

Foreword

Ullin MacBeth was created twelve summers ago in a caravan at the bottom of my garden. If the weather was good I would type out of doors, using a little Imperial Good Companion that had belonged to my father-in-law. The setting for *Ullin MacBeth* was inspired by many wonderful holidays to the island of Mull, situated in the Inner Hebrides of Scotland's ruggedly wild and wonderful west coast.

Nowadays I write in a more civilized fashion, indoors in my study on a word processor, my windows looking out to the beautiful island of Bute and the magical peaks of Arran. But those days spent writing and painting in my caravan were the fun days, even though it was hard work on the little portable, my fingers battered into mush! All those sheets of carbon paper! The Tipp-Ex getting into everything, even my hair.

That is why I remember writing books like *Ullin MacBeth*, not so much the content but the sheer physical graft, and later on, the contentment of a job completed in conditions that were far from perfect.

Christine Marion Fraser

Chapter One

Chrisann pushed her bicycle into the crescent-shaped passing place and propped it against the post at the summit of the hill. The gleaming new machine with its five gears was the very latest model in touring bikes but even so she had been forced to get off more than a mile back and push it up the stiff incline.

Panting slightly from her exertions she swept her mane of silken black hair away from her face with an impatient hand and looked back at the narrow winding road she had just traversed. It lay deserted, dampened by the Scotch mist creeping in from the sea; sheep bleated mournfully from the grassy plateaux which banked up from the shoreline far below. In the distance, to her left, Ben More probed its sullen peak into grey skies, gulping great masses of thick purple cloud into its yawning throat then spewing it out again to let it drift over the forbidding rock in vapour trails that wound lanquidly into deep corries and black rifts of ancient river beds. The massive overhanging cliffs of Gribun glowered menacingly over Loch na Keal, the pitted columns of rock softened by the blurring sea haar.

Despite her fatigue and the sense of being the only person on the island, Chrisann couldn't help being impressed by the sheer overwhelming power of these high places of Mull. She had been here two days now; the weather had been warm, coaxing fragrances of moor and sea into the air. The magic of the Hebrides breathed sweetly from mountain and sky and from the serene friendly faces of the islanders, always ready to raise a hand in greeting or shyly pass the time of day.

The sense of tranquillity reached out to embrace even the animals; buzzards planed majestically on warm air thermals, seemingly intent only in the skilled manoeuvres of flying, rather than in the art of killing; great shaggy Highland cows plodded over white beaches to stand for hours in the cool shallows of the Atlantic; red deer peeped with coy curiosity from cool glades in the forests.

Chrisann's colourful guide book likened Mull to an opal: soft, full of subtle rainbow hues that were sometimes hidden till a trick of light, a ray of sunshine, coaxed out splendours which made you catch your breath with wonder, awe, and sometimes poignancy for a way of life so placid you wanted to stay locked in the enchantment for the rest of your life.

She had camped by the white sands of Calgary, cooking sausages, drinking smoke-flavoured tea, soaking in the peace of the sea. Teeming London seemed a million miles away and so too did Anthony Keats, her agent, who had been shocked and panic-stricken when she had announced her intention of taking some time off from her modelling to come back to Scotland for a holiday.

"My dear Chrisann you simply can't go off just like that," he had told her with a tightening of his already tight lips. "We have a full diary ahead. The thing with Candice was arranged weeks ago and they have settled for a session next week and after that—"

"Anthony, I am having a holiday," she told him firmly. "I'm exhausted and need a break. I told you but you didn't listen. It's all arranged, Mum and Dad are expecting me in Oban tomorrow."

"*Tomorrow!*" His eyes bulged behind his thickly-lensed

spectacles and she had thought he was going to have a fit. "You can't go tomorrow! Raymond Carstairs is coming to do some colour work for—"

"Cancel it – I warned you about Raymond! He thinks everyone should go on their knees when he snaps a finger. I've told him I won't be here tomorrow but he thinks when he's ready everyone else should come running. I also told you several weeks ago I was taking some time off and I'm taking it!"

"Chrisann," Anthony's eyes grew warningly narrow, "you are being very foolish. I don't know what's got into you lately, there's no sparkle left in you, but if it's because of some upset in your private life you mustn't let it show – not in this game."

"It's nothing to do with my private life, I told you, I need a break," she appealed to him. "I'm tired, Anthony, I really am."

"We're all damned tired but don't go running off when the mood takes us! Just because you are successful you think you can do as you please! Remember, I made you what you are, don't ever forget that, my dear."

Her nostrils flared and she lost her temper. "And I had quite a hand in making you what you are, Anthony. Oh yes, I'm front page, middle page, any damned page you care to mention but I didn't get there by sitting back and polishing my fingernails all day long. I've slaved, I've worked till I'm sick of it! I'm fed up being nice to all these cardboard cut-outs you call friends! I'm sick to the teeth of being charming—"

"Charming!" he gritted. "You are a spoiled, pampered little bitch, Chrisann, and you think you can get away with anything. You call my friends false! Well what about you? When I first met you, you were a starry-eyed innocent child, eager to please, beautiful in your simplicity – now – now – you are just as false as anyone else in this business. Out for all you can get. Take! Take! Take! You have become hard, Chrisann, hard as nails . . . and it's showing in your looks."

"Then maybe it's time I had a rest from it all!" she yelled furiously. She put a slender hand up to her forehead and dropped her tone to a silky whisper. "Please, please, darling Anthony, try to understand. I'm washed out, jaded if you like. You're right, I have lost my sparkle. A few days in the country will be the best thing all round, I'll come back refreshed."

His voice became soft, oily. He put a podgy hand on her slim arm. "Of course you need a break, darling, and you will get one next month when things quieten down a bit. Raymond wants to take you abroad – to the sun. He's in love with you and you know it."

"Well I'm certainly not in love with him," she stated firmly. "Oh, he's handsome certainly and very charming – especially when he wants his own way – but I'm not queuing up like all the rest of his girlfriends. I don't need Raymond, thank you very much."

Anthony's eyes had glittered. "Do you need any man, my dear? I've watched you, egging them on then throwing them off when the going gets too hot. Are you afraid of men, Chrisann – or are you as cold as ice under that fiery façade of yours?"

Her cheeks flared. "Mind your own damned business! It's quite a little hobby of yours, ferreting into other folks' affairs. You don't know enough about me and that maddens you, doesn't it? You're ridiculous and stupid too – like all the rest in this business. Not one of the men I've met are genuine. They act their way through life – ten a penny, all of them!"

"Ah yes, falling at your feet, eh, darling? But they soon pick themselves up and run away when they realize they'll never get anywhere with you. I've heard them talking.

With some it's try, try, and try again, the challenge, you know, who will be the first with beautiful Chrisann. Most men like a challenge, others can't be bothered trying – or waiting. With you they'd have to wait forever so if you're not afraid what are you? A little frigid perhaps?"

She had slapped his face then, rage darkening her eyes to midnight violet, and she had spat viciously, "Nine years ago I arrived in London from Scotland, a naïve little seventeen-year-old. I've learned a few things since then, Anthony, learned about people like you for instance. You can't get over the fact that you never got anywhere with me yourself, can you? I was never quite grateful enough to you for starting me off on the right channels. That's it, isn't it? Your silly male pride has taken quite a beating."

"You're a bitch, Chrisann," he had grated, his podgy hand held to his stinging cheek. "A hot-tempered brat. Now, enough of your tantrums, and listen to me, you will be here for Raymond tomorrow and you will keep your appointments with Candice next week. In a week or two you can forget about work for a while when you go off to France with Raymond—"

"No," she said flatly. "It is not Francc with Raymond, it is Scotland with my mum and dad – take it or leave it."

She had flounced to the door but his next words had stopped her. "Chrisann, London is full of girls falling over themselves to get into the modelling game. Young girls, Chrisann, all fresh and dewy-eyed – like you used to be. Oh, I know all the glossies are queuing up to have your beautiful face on their covers – but in two, maybe three years, your phone might not be as hot as it is now – so don't push your luck too far. You be here next week to do those shots for Candice—"

"Let Lorraine do it – she is after all, one of your dewy-eyed young things."

"They want you, Chrisann, so leave your phone number just so I can keep in touch."

The sting of that remembered parting conversation made Chrisann draw in her breath and kick viciously at a clump of bell heather. Damn Anthony! Damn Raymond! Damn them all! But she couldn't damn them out of her existence. When she had arrived at her parents' house in Oban the phone had hardly stopped ringing. First Anthony, his tones too honeyed as he told her he had merely rung to find out if she had arrived safely; then Raymond, peeved because she had left without telling him she was going; Maurice Wiggan, wondering if she would be back in time for a party he was giving in her honour. All the right people would be there, people who wanted to meet her, *so* disappointing for them if she wasn't there. Anthony had given her phone number to everyone she wanted to get away from!

"You *are* popular, Chrisann," her mother had smiled in some bemusement when the phone had once more shattered the peace of the house. Chrisann had been in the lounge enjoying a chat with the big dark man who was her father and she had flounced to the instrument in the hall to listen once more to Raymond's smooth plausible voice telling her how much he missed her, asking when she was coming back.

"I'm not coming back, Raymond!" she had almost shouted down the line. "Not till the week is out."

"But, darling, the colour spread for Sophia," he purred silkily. "Look, should I come up there and do something, try out some new ideas? A few days in Scotland with you might be rather pleasant. We could use some of that Scottish scenery for background. McCaig's Folly might be rather splendid. I could arrange for some of the gang to come, bring a few outfits—"

"No, Raymond, you needn't bother! As a matter of fact I'm moving on for a day or two."

"Moving on? Darling, you can't."

"I can."

"Give me the phone number then." He was only just suppressing his impatience with her.

"Sorry, there won't be one."

"No phone! Come, darling, don't be silly, you must be near a phone."

"Raymond, there are some places in the world where people can get by very nicely without a phone. Don't worry, I'll keep in touch – when it suits me – and don't you dare phone my mother at my home address; she is feeble and getting on and certainly not able to run to the telephone every five minutes. Tell that to Anthony too – and the others." She had slammed the receiver down, cutting off his protests.

Her slim, pretty mother appeared at her side and smiled. "Feeble am I? Getting on – really, Chrisann."

Chrisann laughed and linked her arm through her mother's. "Sorry, I had to say it, Mum, they're vultures and won't leave me alone."

"And where, pray, arc you going now? Dad and I were looking forward to having you till at least the end of the week."

Chrisann sighed. "And I was looking forward to being with you and Dad but I have to have some peace from them – they would come here without notice, you know, and try to talk me into going back with them – and at the moment I don't think I've the strength to resist."

Mrs McNeil looked at her beautiful daughter and saw the dark smudges of weariness under the big violet eyes. "You do look a little tired, Chrisann, I think you work far too hard – where will you go?"

Chrisann was gazing from the window at the shadowed drift of the Mull hills on the horizon. "Mull," she said dreamily.

"Why Mull?"

"Why not? It's an island, I'll get peace there. I'll buy a bike and go camping."

"But you haven't camped since—"

"I was in the Guides. Don't worry, I still remember some of the things I was taught about survival in the wilds – ancient though I may be." She ended with a wry smile lifting the corners of her mouth.

Now she stood on the high lands of Mull, feeling damp, lonely and rather forlorn. The wet air was coaxing out the scents from the harebells, wild thyme, and bell heather which grew in abundance along the roadside. She sniffed the sweetness of the wild flowers and straightened her shoulders. Yesterday she had been looking through her binoculars across Loch Tuath to the small island of Ronnach and she had spotted some derelict dwellings dotted along the shoreline. From an old man on an ancient black bicycle she had extracted some information.

"These are what is left of the crofts the folks were forced to leave during the Clearances," he had told her courteously, his eyes gently absorbing her gleaming bicycle and her brand new track suit which though apt was hardly 'worn in' and stamped her as a novice doing the camping thing for 'a giggle' as Raymond would have put it. In the warm sun of yesterday she had vowed to herself to go over to the island and spend a couple of days exploring but now the idea paled somewhat. She was longing for a hot bath and a proper bed in which she could be sure of a good night's sleep. Bed and Breakfast seemed a good idea but there were no hotels for miles and the only B & B sign had been at a farm a few miles back.

The hum of a powerful engine reached her ears and she saw a mud-splattered Land Rover climbing up the hill towards her. Despite the steepness of the hill the vehicle was coming along at a brisk pace. Chrisann's heart leapt with hope. If she could get a lift, perhaps to the nearest hotel . . . Quite unthinkingly she stepped onto the road, the Land Rover slewed and ground to a halt, the offside front wheel thumped down into a muddy pothole, spraying her with rust-coloured water.

Chrisann gasped and opened her mouth but before she could speak a shaggy blond head was thrust aggressively through the vehicle window and a curt voice demanded, "What the hell do you think you're playing at? I could have killed you just now! It's bad enough trying to avoid the sheep without having to keep an eye open for tourists who float out of the mist from nowhere into the path of oncoming vehicles! Are you lost?"

For a few seconds Chrisann was nonplussed with confusion. But only for a few seconds. In a fury she burst out, "You were driving far too fast to see *anything* let alone me! Pity help the poor sheep who get in your way! How many have you killed in your travels!"

Pushing the hair out of her eyes she looked up and found herself gazing into the most brilliant blue eyes she had ever seen. The anger was receding out of them and in its place was a glint of sardonic amusement. She felt herself flushing as the blue gaze travelled over her in a slow, cool appraisal, taking in every plane and curve of her body. The track suit wasn't the most glamorous apparel, especially now that it was splattered with mud, but it clung to the swell of her breasts and showed to advantage the shapely length of her long slim legs.

He obviously liked what he saw. She could see the amusement deepening in his eyes, lifting the corners of his firm, slightly rebellious mouth, as he said carelessly, "Don't worry about the sheep, I'm always careful where livestock are concerned – but you haven't answered my question – are you lost?"

A surge of irritation shot through her. He had implied

that sheep were more worthy of his consideration than a mere human being. "No, I'm not lost," she told him shortly. "I only wanted to know if there was an hotel nearby."

Again, that infuriating glance of amusement, followed by an incredulous spurt of laughter as he said mockingly, "Hotel? Here, on this road? You'll be lucky. Nearest one is at Dervaig miles back." The blue eyes bored into her and she felt herself beginning to tremble with indignation. He was sizing her up again, looking her over as if she was some prize specimen in a cattle market. She saw that his shoulders were very broad; the deeply bronzed arm leaning easily on the window sill was tightly muscled; the big strong hand looked capable of crushing the life out of anything – yet – the fingers were long and fine. Pity, she mused briefly, if he hadn't been the farm labourer he obviously was those hands might have been capable of better things; an artist, a musician. . . .

"Would you like a lift?" The curt offer broke into her reverie. The tone of his voice put her on her mettle. It implied that she was just a nuisance, someone whom he had encountered and dallied with when he had better things to do with his time.

Her head went up. "No, thank you, I'll have to be getting along, I have quite a way to go."

He gave her a brief nod. "Suit yourself – you probably do it all the time."

He let in the clutch and with a roar of the engine he was off, hurtling away to be lost in the mist. Chrisann felt dismissed, ridiculed, and unaccountably angry. "Lout," she said aloud. "Ill-mannered, uncouth lout."

Determinedly she mounted her bike and pedalled past the head of Loch Tuath. The wind soughed low over the water and she felt a chill creeping through her. She was mad! Mad! Mad! Mad and very wet. Here she was, miles from anywhere and not a living soul in sight. She should have stayed at Calgary with the other campers. Here there were only sheep, sheep, and more sheep, some Highland cows with great horns that terrified her, and dozens of rabbits scampering over the grasslands.

RONNACH FERRY. The signpost pounced at her out of the mist and her heart jumped. Something red loomed in the distance. A phone box. She laughed. A phone box in the middle of nowhere! But convenient. Much more convenient and reassuring than a phone box in the middle of somewhere! She pulled the door open and dialled Oban. Her father answered.

"Are you all right?" he sounded anxious.

"I'm fine, Dad, how's Mum?"

"Worried about you. The mist has come down here."

"Here too."

"Enjoying yourself? Have you got your tent up for the night?"

She paused. "Almost – don't worry, I know an ideal spot. I've had a lovely time, very restful. I'll be home in a couple of days – and I'll try and spend some time with you and Mum before going back to London. Any calls?"

"That Keats chap again."

"Damn him! I told him not to. Look, I'll ring him now, tell him to stop bothering you. Bye, Dad, love to Mum."

She put the phone down and stood fuming. Why couldn't Anthony leave her alone – Raymond too for that matter? But suddenly and contrarily she was filled with longing to hear Anthony nagging at her, pleading with her, letting her know how important she was. It was after all rather nice to be in demand. Here, she was nobody, no one had the least idea she was a successful fashion model. Here everyone was equal, even the very animals had a certain standing: sheep and cows ruled the byways; cars were in the minority and had to give way to the animals.

It was a place where time stood still – the ancient man on the black bicycle seemed to have ambled at her out of the past – he fitted in and was, in his own way, far more superior than she. No one simply knew who she was; farmers and crofters were hardly the sort to go in for glossy women's magazines and she was just another face to them, one of the many visitors who came to the island in the summer. She forgot that the reason she had come to Mull was to capture anonymity and quickly raked through her purse for all the ten pence pieces she could find. She laid them in two high heaps on the shelf and dialled Anthony's home number.

"Darling," his tone was disbelieving, "I've been trying to get in touch. How are you, my sweet?"

She felt a warm glow. "I'm fine, Anthony, enjoying the break. . . ."

"I'm so glad you rang, Chrisann . . ." A frantic bleeping came over the line and she pushed more money into the box. Anthony was still going on. "*Danielle* have been on to me, they want you to do a feature on fashions for next spring. Margo Fawkes, the Fashion Editor has suggested—"

"Anthony, I'm on holiday. I don't want to discuss business right now if you don't mind."

His voice was rising. "I *do* mind, Chrisann, will you damned well stop playing silly games and come back here pronto! I don't know what's got into you, you've never done anything like this before. . . ." His tones became wheedling. "Chrisann, darling, you know you're being unreasonable. . . ."

The bleeps came again and Chrisann cried, "Bye for now, Anthony, I'll be in touch!"

She put the phone down and went outside. The mist

was thicker now and desolation washed over her again. Perhaps Anthony was right, perhaps she was being unreasonable – still, they were all so demanding, all they did was take from her till it seemed she had no strength left. She had to make a stand sometime, after all, she did have a life of her own to lead. She put her cold fingers to her lips and a little frown creased the smoothness of her forehead. What life? Modelling was her life, her whole life; there had to be something more – but what? And whatever it was it seemed an absolute certainty she would not find it on a mist-covered island.

A gull cried overhead, a lost haunting sound. She felt an overwhelming longing to be back in Oban, in her own bedroom, in her own cosy bed, with her mother discreetly fussing and her father, solid and reassuring, listening to her as she talked about her busy life in the city. Sometimes she was aware that he looked at her in a rather bemused fashion. Her life was so far removed from her parents' quiet life in Oban. She had spent seventeen years of her life there yet she felt she didn't belong. London was where she belonged. All her friends were there; her tasteful batchelor girl flat in Kensington was far more familiar to her than her little bedroom in Oban with its camped ceilings and pink wallpaper. At home she was a child again, loved, fussed over, dependent. In London she was somebody, a being in her own right, independent, successful.

The clammy wraiths of sea haar were enclosing her, shutting her into a claustrophobic world. She realized she would have to find somewhere to pitch her tent. A glance at her watch told her it was seven-thirty. Seven-thirty on a July evening in Mull and the sullen grey clouds spraying drizzle over the landscape made it as dark as a night in winter. She rummaged into her saddlebag and taking out a yellow cagoule shrugged herself into it only to discover that the zip was well and truly stuck. “Blast!” she muttered. “Blast! Blast! That’s it! Tonight, Ronnach, tomorrow, home. Chrisann, your days of camping are numbered. You’re a model not a camper – or a cyclist or fresh air fiend for that matter. Tomorrow you go home!”

Chapter Two

The narrow winding track to the jetty was even steeper than the road had been. Chrisann propped her bike against a ramshackle boat shed and glanced around. It was sheltered here in the narrow inlet between Loch Tuath and Loch na Keal but even so she shivered as the mist swirled and curled in over the grey water, seeping into her. Bundles of bright amber seaweed covered the boulder-strewn shore below the jetty; oyster catchers poked and pried among the debris; a frieze of gulls huddled in a decorative row along the length of the cobbled pier, backs to the sea they were silent and dejected looking. A tattered cloud of them drifted beneath the lowering cloud cap on Ronnach, their plaintive cries adding to the sense of isolation.

Out on the placid stretch of water several small boats bobbed, manned by figures in shirt sleeves; a motor launch, white and sleek, rocked gently on its mooring; a few old wooden rowing boats bucked in a ripple of waves slapping round the slimy green steps leading down from the jetty; over by the slipway the sturdy little ferry was tied up in such a way it looked as if it was anchored against a storm.

A group of men were sitting amongst a mountain of lobster pots on rocks which formed the rear of the boat shed. They were talking and laughing quietly as they fiddled with various bits and pieces of fishing gear and they might have been sitting in the bright sunlight of a summer's evening so little effect did the dismal weather have on their spirits. With the exception of one they all sported an assortment of head coverings and it was the exception that caught and held Chrisann's eye for his hair was the colour of ripe wheat. The driver of the Land Rover! He looked up and his eyes held hers for a brief moment before he turned back to the net he was repairing.

She felt an odd sensation of unreality shiver through her. She knew him. Oh, not from that confused meeting on the road back there, from somewhere else. Surely she had seen him sometime before, he was familiar looking in a vague kind of way. Back there on the road she had only glimpsed his face through the mists of drizzle, now she saw his body. He was sitting down but even so she could tell that he was tall, tall and lean and lithe, and she knew somehow that he walked with the careful sure grace of a tiger. . . . She shrugged the feeling off. It couldn't be. He was as much a stranger to her as she obviously was to him. They had met on the road, no more no less.

After that first quizzical glance she held no further interest for him. She walked over to the group. The Exception, as she had mentally christened him, did not look up at her approach but the others, eyes bright with curiosity, watched her with interest.

"Can we help you, lass?" asked a very small man with sinewy arms, a nut brown face, and gentle brown eyes.

Chrisann glanced towards the ferry. "I was wondering – could you tell me what time the ferry leaves for Ronnach?"

The query seemed to amuse the men greatly though inherent politeness quickly brought sobriety to their faces.

"There is no ferry over to Ronnach," explained one or two voices earnestly.

Chrisann was cold and tired and in no mood to be trifled with. The violet of her eyes darkened to storm-cloud purple and she said snappishly, "Of course there is, I can see it with my very own eyes and it said Ronnach Ferry on the sign back there!"

"Ach, it's only a name," said the small man placatingly. "The jetty you are standing on is known by that. The wee ferry you are seeing is only used to take animals and vehicles over to Ronnach. It is not a passenger ferry – Ronnach is private you see," he finished apologetically.

Chrisann ran her long, well-manicured fingers through her hair and felt the hot tears of frustration tightening her throat. "Oh, God," she said despairingly. "I must have somewhere to camp for the night and I *did* want to see Ronnach."

Up till then the blond man hadn't uttered a word but now he looked straight at her and for the second time that evening she found herself gazing into eyes as brilliantly blue as a sun-kissed sea. His face was finely boned, the mouth wide and sensual, his nose was high-bridged and straight, his jawline taut and strong, and his skin was as mahogany brown as that of the other men. But he was different, something set him apart, she didn't know what it was but she sensed it. He was clad in brown cords, wellington boots, and a lovat green, polo-necked jersey, the sleeves of which were rolled to the elbows. His arms were golden brown, furred with blond hair, the muscles of them firm and hard. He was deep chested, powerful looking, yet somehow noble. With a sense of annoyance she felt her heart fluttering and she was unable to tear her eyes away from his cool appraising gaze. He was quite young, in his mid-thirties, perhaps a little older.

"Are you alone?" His voice was deep and cultured but the question was short and sharp. She felt herself bristling and immediately on the defensive. He was ignoring their earlier encounter, as if trying to convey that she was of so little import he didn't remember her at all.

She retorted haughtily, "Oh no! There's a whole army of us. I left the others up on the roadside talking to the sheep!"

His aloof expression didn't flinch, instead he fired another question at her. "How long did you intend to stay on Ronnach?"

"Only a night, I'd like to get back to the mainland tomorrow if possible." Her mouth was stiff with indignation.

"Then it hardly seems worth your while going over to the island, does it?"

His strong brown hands went on repairing the net and she felt very much an intruder.

"And it certainly isn't worth my while staying here to be cross-examined like some criminal!" she fumed at him before turning to flounce back to where she had left her bike. Furiously she pulled it towards her and was in the rather undignified position of having one leg over the saddle when she found her arm in a grip of steel.

"Temper. Temper," the deep cultured voice admonished her with smooth amusement.

"Let go of my arm!" she cried sharply.

"Very well." His grip slackened so suddenly she all but fell off the bike and his arm flashed out again to pull her roughly upright. For a brief moment she was obliged to lean against him and she could feel the lithe muscles rippling in his enclosing arms. He was tall, six feet, if not more. Chrisann was quite tall herself but he loomed above her, dwarfing her, making her feel vulnerable and small. "I'll take you over to Ronnach," he said shortly. She pulled herself away from him.

"You needn't bother!" she spat viciously. "I wouldn't like to put you out on my behalf."

"Don't flatter yourself. I live on Ronnach, I'm going over there now. Bring your bike over to the steps."

A spark of something that might have been described as laughter lit his eyes but it didn't serve to soothe her, instead it made her all the more furious – and somehow humiliated. She had thought the islanders courteous and friendly; this one was neither. How dare he treat her like a bit of flotsam washed in by the tide? She threw herself on her bike and began to pedal away. On the shore a curlew bubbled out its haunting song. She turned her head to look back. Ronnach lay green and peaceful under its fluffy covering of cloud; the boats bobbed serenely; seaweed waved lazily in the shallows. She *wanted* to go over to Ronnach, somehow she wanted it more than she had ever wanted anything else in her life. Perhaps the very idea that it was private made it all the more fascinating. She didn't know or care, she pined to set foot on it.

That backward glance was her undoing, for in her sweeping appraisal of the scene she took in the man with the wheat-coloured hair. He was etched against the backdrop of Ronnach, tall, powerful, compelling, filling the screen of her vision.

The Exception! The Exception. The words rang in her head. He didn't turn round to see if she was following. He strode towards the slimy green steps and began to climb down.

Damn you! I *will* come! She thought swiftly.

He looked up now but not at her. "Are you coming, Colin Mor?" He called.

"Ay, be right with you, Ullin." The small man detached himself from his cronies and walked towards the steps.

Ullin! The big man was called Ullin. Unusual, but then, he was not the usual type of man, different, The Exception. When she reached the steps the man named Colin Mor was settling his neat frame on a thwart which was almost hidden among a jumble of ropes and oilskins. The big man glanced up at Chrisann's approach and stretched out his arms. But they weren't for her. "Hand down the bike," he said curtly.

Her gaze travelled down the greasy steps to the deep black water slapping against the side of the big rowing boat. The sight made her heart lurch. "Hand down the bike," he said again, as if he was talking about a feather. She doubted she would get herself down those treacherous steps let alone haul down a bike laden with gear.

She swayed on the edge of the cobbles, overcome by an attack of giddiness. He remained unmoving, like a big bronze statue with upstretched arms, the blue eyes glinting with amusement. Anger lent her strength. She grabbed hold of the bike and staggered as she set one cautious foot on the top step. Colin Mor's gentle brown eyes became startled at the sight of her struggling to get both herself and the bike down into the boat. With great agility he scuttled the length of the boat and up the steps in a flash.

"Here, let me take that, Miss," he offered with lilting gallantry in his voice. "I did not know you were coming over or I would not have got into the boat first."

No, but *he* knew, she thought furiously, but she did not demean herself by voicing what was in her mind. Colin Mor was small but strong and in seconds he had carried her bike down. It was while he was arranging the awkward shape of it across the hull that the flap of the saddlebag flipped open and out rolled a tin of dried milk and a packet of sugar. They made only a small splash as they went into the water and careered to the depths. Chrisann stared. She must have left the flap undone whilst searching for her jacket. It was her own fault but the knowledge of that didn't make it easier. The one thing she had been looking forward to was a cup of hot, sweet tea. She bit her lip. It seemed the last straw. The night stretched endlessly ahead, full of damp mist, tinned soup, and black tea which she hated.

"I'm right sorry, Miss." It was Colin Mor, apologizing in his soft voice.

"It's – it's all right, Colin, my own fault." She forced lightness into the words. The last thing she wanted was for the big man to see how upset she was at the loss of her precious rations. She had reached the last three slippery steps. The boat lurched and jumped away from the wall leaving four feet of black deep space. In panic she stared down at the water frisking and splashing over the steps to her feet. Strong hands caught hers and terror choked her as she thought for one terrible moment she was going to be pulled into the sea. Then she was flying through space, being caught and steadied in an embrace so protective there might have been intimacy in it if it hadn't been so brief.

For a split-second her hands lay in his strong brown ones, the warmth of his body beat into hers, she smelled the faint aroma of aftershave. Almost roughly he pushed her away and told her to sit on a thwart at the stern. He went to the oars and began to pull steadily away from the jetty. The rhythmic sound of paddles beating water was so soothing she felt mesmerized by it.

Absently she watched the dirty water swirling round inside the boat. Before she had time to act it slopped over her immaculate white plimsoles, soaking them, creeping through her socks to her feet. Folding her cold hands under her armpits she watched Ronnach growing nearer, saw the sheep dotted over the undulating grey-green hills. She was aware of its nearness, even as she was aware of the man at the oars. She glanced at him. He seemed lost in thought, his eyes gazing at some point above her head.

"You're from the town." The sudden statement was like an accusation.

"I work in London," she said coldly, then, as if to recompense for that admission she added defensively, "but I'm from Oban originally."

His eyes swept over her and she was acutely aware that her careful grooming of the morning made her look as if she was posing for the front page of a sporting glossy. Her blue, well-fitting track suit was unstained, except for the splashes on the legs made by *his* Land Rover. Her white polo-necked sweater was spotless, her long nails gleamed from a recent application of pearly nail varnish, her hair though damp still retained its style, thanks to expert shaping. Except for a touch of slate-grey eyeshadow and glossy liptint she wore no make-up, the pure, milky whiteness of her skin didn't need it and was a compliment to the night-black of her hair.

But under the cool indifference of his appraisal she felt pale, an exotic plant which had spent too much of its life under glass and was therefore unable to take the harsh realities of the great outdoors. She could almost feel him thinking these things and anger rose in her because he made her feel unsure of herself – and somehow inferior.

After that first observation he appeared to have nothing further to say. Colin Mor smiled shyly at her from his place at the bow. He only had two teeth at the front but rather than dating him they gave him the appearance of a bashful small boy. His skin was soft and dewy, his brown eyes full of a timid friendliness. Chrisann felt her heart warming to him. She wondered what would have happened if he hadn't come to her rescue back there on the jetty. Surely the big man would have eventually unbended and come to her aid? After all, it was only common courtesy for any man to give a helping hand to a woman.

He was pulling at the oars, purposefully, silently, the sinews of his arms tensing like steel rope. He wasn't any man, he was 'the Exception', arrogant, self-assured, compelling, seemingly without manners – yet – he had helped her jump into the boat – no – hauled her in more like because he had grown impatient and wanted to be on his way.

It began to rain harder, a steady drizzle that blotted out Ronnach and the Mull shores. The oars slapped. Slap! Slap! The water slid past, grey-green. She felt her world was confined to a boat, a small patch of sea, and two men who were as silent as the blotted-out hills.

"Just a wee bit to go, Ullin," Colin Mor spoke suddenly. "You get along up to the house. I'll see to the boat. Jean will have put a match to your fire seeing it's so damp at night."

A fire! Chrisann couldn't suppress a pang of longing. How lovely to sit at a cosy fire with someone to talk to and share a meal with. But there was no one like that here. Raymond flashed into her mind, tall, dark, over-talkative, charming when he wanted to be, suave, sophisticated, how different from . . . with a start she realized she had been about to compare Raymond with this man – Ullin. She had only just met him and she was wishing she could share his fire. Met him! Encountered would be a more accurate description of their brush on the jetty and her only reasons for pining for a seat by his cosy fire was because on this drab evening it seemed to her she was deprived of every kind of comfort she had always taken for granted before.

The rain was driving into her, soaking through the cagoule to her sweater, her feet felt like two lumps of lead. The jetty loomed into view but they went on past it towards the shore. The keel crunched on shingle and Colin Mor scrambled out, splashing through the water in wellingtons that looked too big for his short legs. The big man shipped the oars to join his companion and between them they pulled the boat half out of the water. Chrisann was thankful she wouldn't have to contend with more slimy steps. The jetty was small and obviously kept clear for the ferry.

The man called Ullin was lifting the bike from the boat, setting it on its side against a big boulder. Colin Mor was talking to a plump little woman who had emerged from a whitewashed house some way up from the shoreline. Chrisann sat where she was at the stern of the boat which was surrounded by water so clear she could see little red sea anemones waving their tentacles among pink, green, and white stones. The big man had joined Colin Mor and the woman they were calling Jean.

Chrisann sat and fumed. The great blond brute obviously had no intention of helping her out of the boat. If she stepped out from the side she would be up to her eyes in water. She was exaggerating the situation out of all proportion she knew but she felt so shut out from the intimate little group talking together outside the whitewashed house that self-pity was getting the upper hand of reason. Abruptly she stood up and tried to make her way to the bow but the vessel tilted and she found herself with one leg over the side, the water lapping over her knee. In a flurry of indignation she brought her other leg over and waded to the shore, feeling tears of rage welling into her eyes. Colin Mor turned and saw her predicament and concern flashed into his gentle eyes.

"Ach, Miss!" he cried, hurrying down to take her hand and help her over the stony beach. "You should have waited," he reprimanded quietly. "I was just asking my wife to put the kettle on and make you some tea. Will you come in and dry yourself?"

Chrisann felt ridiculous and humiliated and when she caught the look of amusement in the blond man's blue eyes she couldn't control her burst of outrage. "Thank you, but no! I'll just get my bike and go." She stamped over to the machine and hauled it upright. As she crunched it over the stones to the tarred track her shoes squelched water and the plump woman looked at her with concern. "Ach, Miss, you're wet through," she said softly. "Are you sure you wouldn't like to come in for a wee while? There's a nice fire going and a pot of broth keeping warm. You could be doing fine with some of that."

Chrisann felt herself weakening. She was cold and so tired her limbs felt heavy. The offer was tempting, the kindly manner of Colin Mor and Jean a balm to her ruffled spirits. She opened her numb lips to accept the invitation but a curt "Wait" made her turn to see the blond man lifting a bundle of waterproofs from the boat. With slow and measured stride he came over to her and pushed the things at her. "Take these." He made it sound like a command. "You'll find them of more use to you than . . ." his gaze swept over her and she bristled, " . . . these flimsy things you have on. When you've done with them you can hand them into Jean here."

All her urges made her want to hurl the waterproofs straight into his handsome, arrogant face but he was walking away, up the track, bidding Colin Mor and Jean good-night. Chrisann threw the bundle of fish-smelling oils over the handlebars of her bike and set out to follow the tall, retreating figure.

"Wait!" she cried. "Where do I camp?"

He stopped so abruptly she almost collided with him. His blue gaze was directly upon her and her heart jumped strangely. She knew him! From somewhere she knew him. But where? Where? She matched his gaze with an unwavering one of her own. Although his hair was wet and his pullover fuzzed with rain he was not the least concerned. He blended agreeably with the green fields, accepted the wiles of weather without fuss. Bronzed and startlingly handsome, he looked in full possession of himself. He stood beside her yet was remote from her, remote and cool, in control of his emotions. She felt he was the sort who didn't let life rule him. He was in the reigning seat, a king within his kingdom, his subjects obeying him yet never resenting it because he commanded too much respect and affection from them.

Chrisann was rather alarmed by these odd thoughts and fancies that crowded into her head. How silly of her! He was a boorish brute with no manners. Was it only with strangers he was so abrupt – or did he ever give anything of himself to anybody?

With a nod of his head he indicated the road snaking away into the mist. "Best set your tent on the other side of the island. It isn't far. Ronnach is not very wide. You won't be in the way there. We're busy with the clipping just now and the fanks are on this side."

She wasn't so out of touch with country ways that she didn't know 'fanks' was the island word for sheep pens. "I'll only be here one night so I can assure you I won't upset your sheep," she said coldly.

He nodded again. "Good. I'll bid you good-night then."

He turned away from her and went towards a gate set in a drystone wall that ran the length of the road. She watched him go, the long agile legs taking him swiftly and surely through grass studded with rain diamonds. The mist swirled and lifted slightly and she saw in the distance a sturdy grey stone house set against a gentle sloping hillside. In itself the house might have presented a rather drab appearance in the grey landscape but a light glowed warmly from a downstairs window and it looked cosy and welcoming. This then was where he lived. If it hadn't been for his attire he might have been some Nordic giant silhouetted elusively on the brow of the misted field, his hair a pale helmet of gold.

She sensed that he turned his head slightly to look at her before he disappeared from view in a hollow and now she was alone again only this time there were feelings in her breast that hadn't been present before her arrival at Ronnach Ferry; feelings of rejection, hurt, and desolation, mixing together to form a potion that seemed to seep through every part of her, making her feel so bewildered she wasn't aware that she was walking on again, pushing the bike to the other side of the island 'out of the way'!

She found a lush table of grassland and pitched her tent in the lee of a heather-covered outcrop of rock. Under cover of the gay blue and orange tent, with her feet dry and beginning to warm up inside a pair of thick woolly socks, she began to feel better. Opening a tin of tomato soup she set it to heat on her little Calor gas stove. When it was piping hot she tipped it into a big mug and leaving it to cool slightly she buttered a roll and a piece of crispbread. Sitting on her bed roll with the mug between her hands, feeling the soup glowing through her, her former feelings of self-pity began slowly to dissipate.

Absently she gazed through the open tent flap, letting her thoughts wander, but no matter how hard she tried to discipline them they came back in the end to the big man with wheat-coloured hair, the man known only to her as Ullin. What had he thought of her with her fancy bike and her inexperience with weather and boats? Had he seen her as someone trying hard to look the part of an explorer, or as a nosy tourist, a stranger and a nuisance – had he seen her at all? She shook herself in annoyance. What on earth was she thinking about, thinking about him? He was nothing to her, a mere ship she had passed in the night and would most likely never see again. He was no one, no one of importance in her life, a total stranger, nothing more. But was he? The feeling that she had met him before persisted no matter how hard she tried to shake it off.

She went outside and scrambled over the shore to wash her mug and soup pan in the sea. The haar had lifted to form a strange overhead blanket. The water was calm, the air salt-laden. Harebells and wild rock plants grew in abundance everywhere, even on the odd patches of grass among the stones on the shore. Out on the horizon a blue, ethereal shape appeared. Staffa! It must of course be Staffa of Mendelssohn's famous Hebridean Overture, Fingal's Cave.

About nine yards in front of her a black, shiny head popped out of the water and a huge pair of meltingly beautiful and inquisitive dark eyes gazed at her. Chrisann put her fingers to her lips and for a long moment she held the gaze of the grey, Atlantic seal. It put its nose into the air and sniffed, its whiskers bristled forward, then with a languid toss of its flippers it dived out of sight. Chrisann gave a little chuckle of delight. She was on Ronnach, seeing Staffa, watching Atlantic seals watching her. She wasn't hungry or cold any more. Anthony and Raymond were mere shadows in her memory. Other things filled her mind, other people. Ullin! Ullin! Not a shadow but a powerful, compelling, and oddly disturbing presence in her head.

She left the water's edge and walking round the other side of 'her' rocky outcrop she discovered a little stream tinkling over smooth boulders to form a tiny waterfall. Going back to the tent she collected her toilet bag and washed her face and cleaned her teeth in the fresh, cold water. It was lovely, so lovely she put her mouth to a gurgling waterspout to take a deep draught of the pure sweet 'Uisge-Beatha', the Gaelic name for the 'water of life'; though more often that name was fondly bestowed on whisky rather than on plain water. She gasped and choked as it tumbled over her face and trickled inside the collar of her jersey. It didn't matter. It was bedtime.

She went back to the tent and changing quickly into pyjamas she crawled inside her sleeping bag and zipped it up. The airbed was soft beneath her. She felt warm and comfortable and more relaxed than she had felt for a long time. The sea sighed and hushed nearby; it was like a soothing lullaby and her eyes began to close. She was on Ronnach. If the mist had lifted by morning she would perhaps stay long enough to explore the place. There was no need, absolutely no reason for running away from the island just because a big blond man called Ullin had told her she mustn't get in the way of the sheep.

Chapter Three

At just after eight the next morning Chrisann looked out of the tent and felt her heart sinking at sight of dismal drizzle blotting out everything but a few feet of grass surrounding the tent. If anything the mist was thicker than ever with not even the sea visible. Shutting the flaps quickly she crawled back inside to rummage through her small supply of stores to see what she could drum up for breakfast. The idea of black tea or coffee was totally repulsive to her but at least she could have a buttered roll and an egg, washed down with fresh spring water. The egg was boiling merrily in the pan when she heard footsteps swishing through the grass and a soft tuneless whistle. Her heart leapt. Surely not the 'Nordic Giant' come to make his apologies for his behaviour of the previous evening – or was he coming to check up on her, make sure she was behaving herself on private land? It wasn't Ullin, it was Colin Mor rustling with oilskins, pink face aglow, his toothy grin coming shyly after his first tentative, "Are you awake yet, Miss?"

"Good-morning, Colin Mor," she greeted him, genuinely pleased to see him.

"To you as well, Miss, though hardly a good description of such a dreich day." He fumbled in his pockets, from one extracting a carton of long-life milk, from the other a bag of sugar. "Jean sent these, I told her yours had landed in the sea and she made me come up with them first thing."

Chrisann took the packages gratefully. "Bless you both, now I can make some coffee. Will you stay and have a cup with me?"

He debated the offer for a considerably long minute, obviously so overcome with shyness he couldn't make up his mind whether to go or stay. In the end he said off-handedly, "Ach well, just for a wee while, I've got to look in on Mr MacBeth on the way back."

With much rustling he crawled inside the tent and small though he was the already confined space shrank to embarrassingly limited proportions. He was literally rubbing shoulders with Chrisann and a blush spread over his already rosy cheeks. She pretended not to notice and popped on the little kettle-cum-teapot. While waiting for it to boil she put coffee and sugar into a cup for herself and the same into her own mug for Colin who took "Two wee sugars, thank you, and no' very much coffee."

"Mr MacBeth," she said carelessly, "does he live nearby?"

"Ay, in the grey house over from the road. He's a grand man is Ullin."

Ullin MacBeth! She had his full title now, at least she could put a name to the aloof creature with hair the colour of ripe wheat and blue eyes that tormented her with their expression of mocking amusement. From history lessons at school she knew that MacBeth had been a Celtic King of Scotland, reigning way back in the eleventh century. She remembered her notions of the night before and wondered musingly if the arrogance and pride of nobility had somehow carried on down the ages to be born in one Ullin MacBeth of the twentieth century. She also recalled learning that MacBeth meant the 'lively one' in Gaelic. She wasn't acquainted enough with Ullin MacBeth to know if that description applied to him or not. Those blue eyes were certainly alert enough, missing nothing, seeing everything with an unnerving detachment.

"Mrs MacBeth is very lucky, living in such a lovely place. I'm not seeing it at its best but when the sun shines it must be paradise." She was fishing but she had to know. Colin Mor's honest face took on a closed look.

"Mr MacBeth lives alone, Miss," he said evasively and Chrisann was mad at herself for letting her curiosity rule her better senses. He got up to go, at the door of the tent murmuring a polite, "Thank you for the coffee, Miss."

"You're very welcome, Colin Mor," she said warmly. "And it's I who should thank you for bringing the milk and sugar." She laughed. "I also should apologize to you and your wife for my bad manners of yesterday. You were so kind, offering me shelter and food and I was very rude to both you and Jean. I hope you've forgiven me."

His smile beamed out once more. "Ach, none of us are at our best when we are cold and tired; think nothing more about it."

Chrisann glanced up at the dismal sky. "Will this mist last much longer, do you think? If there was a chance of it blowing away I would love to stay on for a day or two."

"Ach well, there's no knowing really, Miss, but," he grinned perkily, "much as I don't like it I don't much fancy a storm either."

"Do you think there's one coming then?" she asked anxiously.

He nodded wisely. "Maybe not, but often a wind is the only thing to shift a haar like this and sometimes it just forgets to hold its breath and can get real wild with us all."

He went off chuckling and Chrisann returned to her belated breakfast. The rain came down harder around mid-morning and she sat on her bed roll, hugging her knees, listening to the steady drumming. She ought to pack up and go home but how awful to strike camp in the downpour and roll up a sodden tent. She would get soaked with everything else for she had no intention of donning the thick rubber waterproofs that Ullin MacBeth had thrown at her.

She looked at them lying in a heap in a corner of the tent; the yellow trousers were dirty and tar-stained, the orange jacket not much better. They were no doubt utterly practical but she loathed the idea of putting them on. What a sight she would look muffled to the ears in dirty, fish-smelling oils, which undoubtedly would be miles too big for her – then a thought struck her. Last night Ullin MacBeth had walked up the road with drizzle soaking through his clothes; hard though he was he had sacrificed his waterproofs to a total stranger while he himself got wet. The realization brought a strange glow to her heart. She had imagined him to be without manners or feelings yet he had enough of both to concern himself like that. A hard man with a soft centre! She would take the things back to him today – now – this very minute!

He was obviously a man who went about in all weathers; how awful that he should get soaked because of her. Not that she particularly wanted to see him again, the very opposite in fact. His manner towards her last night had brought out the very worst in her and there was no doubting that she had left him with a bad impression of her. As if that mattered, of course. She hadn't the least intention of trying to impress upon him that she wasn't all tantrums and bad temper because she suspected he was not at all the sort to be taken in by feminine wiles.

In fact, she shrank from seeing again the mocking contempt in those blue eyes; it was only common decency that urged her to go back to him and return the waterproofs. Thus she argued with herself as she hastily donned her yellow cagoule and made her way outside. The blast of rain against her face was somewhat repelling but resolutely she bundled the oils over her arm and trudged through the sodden grass to the road. One or two gates led into fields but a quarter way along she noticed a wooden gate set into the wall and she reckoned it must lead to the house she had glimpsed last night. She pushed and it stuck which meant it was seldom used. A stronger push sent it scraping open.

Head bent against the driving rain she went through and walked straight into a pot-hole filled with muddy water which reached up over her shoes to soak the bottom of her track suit.

"Oh, no," she groaned. "Ullin MacBeth, you'd better be worth all this."

A rutted track wound from the gate over a field cropped so short it resembled a well-kept lawn. Topping the rise she saw the grey house standing aloofly against the hill. At close quarters there were signs of homeliness. Paths had been made and scattered with stones brought up from the shore. Rock plants grew unchecked over them and made a beautiful natural carpet of colour; hens crooned and pecked in every corner; on a windowsill by the door a black and white cat was diligently washing its face; on another ledge a fat brown hen roosted amongst pots of geraniums; beneath an old table outside the coalshed, a group of chaffinches picked at breadcrumbs, quite unconcerned by the presence of the nearby cat.

The scene was so typically Hebridean that Chrisann couldn't suppress a little chuckle of delight. On her travels in Mull she had come across many such examples of harmonious relationships among the animals. At a garden in Dervaig she had witnessed the frolics of five orange kittens playing with two adult cats whilst a budgie in a cage nearby chirped happily in the sun. The motto seemed to be 'live and let live'. The wild rabbits in the fields were so unconcerned by human intrusion their only acknowledgement of it as such was to freeze for a few seconds before hopping a few paces to get on with the business of eating.

She went up to the door and knocked. There was no answer. Even as she knocked again she knew no one was at home. Something moved in the distance, two figures were receding into the rain, one small and sturdy, the other a tall giant with hair the colour of ripe wheat; beside them ran the black and white shape of a sheep-dog. Both men were like spectres, mere blurs against the rain-washed sky but even so she could not mistake them for any other but Colin Mor and Ullin MacBeth.

Disappointment washed over her with such unexpected intensity she felt cheated and she leaned against the door jamb to watch till the men were out of sight. Angry at herself she jerked herself upright and was about to stuff the waterproofs into an old empty meat safe by the door when she thought better of it and snatched them back into her arms once more. If she did nothing else during her miserable stay on Ronnach she would return those waterproofs to Ullin MacBeth – personally.

She spent a solitary but peaceful day, enjoying the sound of the sea, the call of seabirds, the bleating of sheep, intense and constant all over the island. By late afternoon, Colin Mor's weather predictions were coming to fruition. The wind was meek enough to begin with but by the time Chrisann had eaten and was washing her dishes in the burn, it had risen to a gale that keened in over the sea, lashing the waves into white horses that bucked and frisked over the grey-green swell. The mist was rising, swirling, dispersing before the onslaught, piling up to join slate-blue clouds racing beneath an angry ochre sky. Staffa appeared, remote and mysterious; to the right of it one or two dark shadows: the islands of the Treshnish group.

It was so wildly beautiful Chrisann walked to a nearby headland to stand on the cropped turf and let the wind buffet her. It plucked at her slim figure, grabbed at the unzipped cagoule and puffed it into a yellow balloon. A roguish gust tore off her hood and her hair was whipped around her face like strands of black silk. She laughed aloud. She felt good; free; alive. In the last few months she had walked, talked, slept, worked – like a robot! She had felt no joy, little satisfaction in anything she did. Now she was so infected by the exuberance of the weather she spread her arms and whirled round like a child dancing with happiness.

So entranced was she, that she didn't notice the storm clouds were thickening; purple and green they massed together to join forces for a mighty spectacular. The first rains swept in over the sea, rubbing out the distant islands, bringing a wind that screeched through the heather and plucked the surface from the water, tossing it into angry violence. Chrisann was almost blown from her feet.

Staggering she leaned into the wind and began to run for the shelter of the tent. But she was soaked before she reached it. Gasping and almost drowned she was blown towards the rocky outcrop where to her utter dismay she found the tent had ripped from its moorings and lay in a bedraggled heap over a jagged rock. All her belongings, clothes, bedding, food supply were exposed to the unmerciful cloudburst. Chrisann stared in horrified disbelief. The ground was waterlogged and all that she needed for survival was half-submerged in water.

Although it was just after nine the lowering skies had brought early darkness and she fell to her knees to fumble for her torch. But it was dead, rain-filled and useless. Torrents of rain lashed into her. She clasped her hands round her shoulders and began to tremble in a mixture of cold and dread. What on earth could she do? She was alone – who was there to turn to? Before the answer had time to gel in her mind she was on her feet, running over the grass to the road, the wind buffeting her, the rain lashing her, stinging her face, blinding her so that she hardly saw where she was going.

A great swelling sound reached her, tossed at her out of the wind: sheep bleating mournfully, discordant grunts, raucous yells. She stumbled and fell into a roadside ditch which flowed like a miniature river.

"Damn!" she sobbed, scrabbling at roots and ferns, eventually hauling herself out of the freezing water.

A gate loomed and she ran to push it open. A moving grey-white sea met her eyes. Sheep! Hundreds of them huddled together; pushing; jostling; jumping over each other. She ran back onto the road and looked wildly about. In the distance a light wavered, disappearing, re-appearing according to the whims of a straggle of storm-wracked trees. She opened another gate and sped towards the light. It grew bigger and brighter as she drew closer – a beacon in a storm. She went to the same door she had knocked on earlier and beat it with her fists, almost falling into the arms of Ullin MacBeth who wrenched it open.

"What the hell . . .?" His deep voice was like music in her ears. She forced herself to be calm and somehow as dignified as possible with rivers of rain running down her face. He was standing with his back to the light and she only knew it was him by his height and the outline of pale gold round his head – 'like a halo'; the fancy strayed into her head and her heart lightened a little.

"I'm very sorry to bother you," she had meant to sound

unconcerned and was surprised when the words came out in a gasp. "My tent has blown down and – and—"

"Come inside! For heaven's sake, don't just stand there, girl!" His hand came out to grip her arm and pull her roughly indoors. "In here." He propelled her forward and she was too exhausted and miserable to resist or voice a protest of any sort. She found herself in a fairly large room which was lit only by an oil lamp and the flames of a fire piled high with peats. The walls were lined with bookshelves; a huge chintz sofa with two matching chairs were parked invitingly round the fire; on the hearthrug a black and white collie looked up at Chrisann with wary brown eyes though its tail thumped the floor.

Ullin MacBeth wasted no time in preliminary small talk. He pushed Chrisann into a chair by the fire and went out of the room, coming back in minutes with a big fluffy towel. "Here, dry yourself," he commanded.

Chrisann's teeth were beginning to chatter. She took the towel and began to rub her face with it but with an impatient grunt he seized it from her and bending over her enveloped her head inside it, rubbing briskly. She felt like a small girl, if not exactly cosseted at least taken charge of to some degree. It was rather unreal, not so long ago she had been battling against a storm, now, in a short space of time, she was seated by Ullin MacBeth's fire and he was drying her hair.

"You finish off." He let the towel crumple into her lap. Going over to a big mahogany sideboard he opened a door and taking out a bottle of whisky and a glass, poured a good measure. He came back to stand beside her, tall, looming, filling the room with his presence. "Drink this."

She shook her tousled head. "No, I don't."

"You'll drink it if you know what's good for you."

She took the glass and swallowed some of the amber liquid, spluttering and coughing, grimacing at the taste.

"There, that wasn't so bad, was it?" His voice held undertones of sarcasm and she felt the old anger rising up against him. "You needn't have gotten into this state you know," he said heavily and she glared up at him, sparks flying out of her darkening eyes. "Not if you'd had the sense to wear the waterproofs I gave you."

She started guiltily. He was right! Of course he was right. And the waterproofs had been in the tent which had blown over, exposing everything to the weather. "I'm sorry," she hated herself for stammering slightly, "I came to give them back to you this morning but you were out."

"I didn't need them but you did. These were the ones I keep in the boat, I have spares here – of all the stupid women I've met you take some beating!"

"Don't you dare call me stupid – or compare me to your other women – I don't happen to be one of them!" She was on her feet, shouting at him, her fists clenching at her sides.

A small worried whine came from the dog's throat. "Quiet, Mirk, quiet, boy," his master soothed. "Everything's all right."

"Everything is *not* all right!" she stormed, throwing the towel to the floor and all but stamping on it. She pushed the glass of whisky at him, slopping some of it over his brown Shetland wool sweater. "Thank you for your Highland hospitality, Mr MacBeth – what there was of it! I'll get out of your road now, leave you and your dog in peace!"

She flounced to the door, wrenched it open, and ran down the dark passageway leading to the outer door. But he was there before her, taking her wrists in a vice like grip, forcing her to bend her arms till her fists were touching her shoulders. She fought him like a wildcat, her body arched and contorted, her wet hair falling over her face. He was so near her she could smell again that faint, pleasing aroma of aftershave, see the firm determined mouth tightening as she lashed out at him with her feet.

"You little vixen!" he gasped. "Hot-tempered, spoiled little bitch!"

His teeth flashed and with horror she saw that he was enjoying the tussle.

"Let me go." Her breath was ragged in her throat. "What kind of man are you? I can't think why Colin Mor has such a high opinion of you. A fine man indeed! There's nothing at all fine about you. You're a boorish brute!"

She expected him to make some angry retort but the sensual mouth merely lifted with amusement.

"There are times when any man's finer feelings are overshadowed by other instincts," he said mockingly.

"Just what do you mean by that?"

He said nothing for a moment but just stood gazing down at her till it seemed his eyes were searing into her mind, reading her innermost thoughts. Chrisann was so conscious of his nearness, the virile power of his body, that her heart pounded and she felt faint.

"You're hurting my arms," she whispered weakly. "Let me go this minute."

She began to struggle again and saw at once that it was her undoing. Ullin MacBeth had her against the wall now, pinning her arms above her head, the brutal strength of him rippling the muscles in his arms, tightening the sinews. She could see the pulse beating in his neck – very fast – with excitement. All the strength left her and she went suddenly limp.

"Don't – oh please – don't," she sobbed.

He let her go and stood back to stare at her. His handsome face was a blur in the soft flood of light from the living-room doorway.

"You little idiot," he breathed harshly, anger replacing the amusement in his eyes. "What the hell do you think I am? A sort of all-conquering caveman from the Prehistoric times? Again you flatter yourself! This isn't a sex tussle, damn you! I was only trying to stop you making a fool of yourself again. Did you *really* think I was going to sit back and let you run off into the night? Did you?"

Chrisann shook her head, reaction lightening her head so much she felt giddy. "I don't know, Mr MacBeth. You might have done. You certainly showed little concern for me before. I'm – I'm sorry I behaved so foolishly just now – it was just . . ."

"It's just that you *are* a hot-headed ass, that's what! Now, get a hold of yourself this minute and stop your nonsense. You will have a hot bath and change into some dry clothes while I go out and see if I can fix your tent. Is that clear?"

She nodded dumbly and he disappeared up a flight of stairs at the top of the passageway. Coming back he dumped a pile of clothes into her arms. "Use these – the bathroom is upstairs – the door's at the end of the hall."

He turned abruptly from her and going to the outer porch shrugged himself into a yellow waterproof suit. Mirk slunk out of the living-room, to look appealingly at his master. "No, Mirk, go back." The order was firm but kindly and the dog obediently turned and went back into the warmth of the living-room. "If only people were as sensible," muttered Ullin MacBeth and Chrisann knew that it was only out of politeness he hadn't said 'women'. A lantern flashed, the door opened and shut and he was gone.

She clutched the bundle of clothes to her breast and thought wryly that she was getting into the habit of accepting other people's garments. Rather unsteadily she made her way upstairs, her mind racing. That man! He was impossible! Rude, a bully . . . a – a brute!

She reached the bathroom and pushed open the door. It was small but modern with a turquoise suite and a shower in one corner. On the window ledge was a jumble of male toiletries, on the bath bar a tasteful assortment of bath salts, body cologne, talcum; hanging from the wrought iron screen that divided the bath from the wash basin was a pink fluffy powder puff together with a shower cap and a pretty pink toilet bag. All very feminine and frivolous. But of course! Ullin MacBeth might live on a remote island but that didn't mean he was celibate. A man like him didn't go through life without female companions – strings of them no doubt. Despite that aloof exterior he had the same needs – the same wants as any other strong, virile man.

Her consternation at the realization that he obviously shared his home with some woman was so intense she forgot for the moment how much she hated him for his arrogance, and his bad manners. What had made her assume that a man of his calibre could possibly reach his stage in life totally unnoticed by the women he had passed along the way?

Chrisann, you *are* a fool, she silently scolded herself as she fingered the feminine display on the shelves. Who did they belong to? His wife? The idea of that utterly dismayed her. Colin Mor had been very evasive on that score. If he *was* married where was his wife? The things more probably belonged to his lover – or lovers – lots of them. . . . She shook herself angrily. What did she care? He could have a whole harem if he liked. It mattered not one bit to her.

She picked up a large bottle of bubble bath and uncorked it. His wife or lover wouldn't miss some of this. She poured a large dollop of it into the bath, smiling with satisfaction as she did so, then she turned the hot water tap. The water gurgled and splashed, bubbles piled up to make a perfumed foam, steam rose in clouds. Taking off her wet clothes she stepped into the bath. It was delicious, soothing, relaxing her into a state of calm.

She soaked for longer than she intended for she meant to be dressed and back downstairs before the return of Ullin MacBeth. The clothes he had given her were like new, the camel cord slacks and soft blue angora jumper fitting her perfectly. She felt warm and refreshed but rather resentful of the woman in Ullin MacBeth's life with her excellent taste in clothes and her toiletries intimately rubbing shoulders with his.

Hanging her wet things neatly on a clothes airer she placed it over the bath. It would never do to have her things dripping rain over the floors. She would let that rude creature see that whatever else she lacked he could not add sloppiness to his list.

Downstairs in the living-room it was warm and quiet and luckily Ullin wasn't back. Mirk wagged his tail from his place on the rug and allowed her to make friendly advances towards him. The room was full of atmosphere, lived-in without being shabby. The brasses on hearth and mantelshelf gleamed. Jean's work thought Chrisann, or – the woman whose clothes she was wearing now. She ran her hands over the collection of books, all kinds, novels, a collection of clan histories, poetry, something to suit most tastes. The peats glowed warmly in the grate; a 'wag at the wa' clock lazily swung the time away; Mirk breathed gently, one ear cocked in the direction of the door; the rain hissed against the window panes but it was muffled by heavy drapes, shut out, belonging to another world.

Chrisann sat down on one of the chintz chairs. It was soft and comfortable and smelt faintly of pipe smoke, the fragrant sort; there was also a lingering of aftershave on the head rest – this was *his* chair. She could picture him relaxing in it, his lithe body at ease, his pipe in his mouth, Mirk's head resting on his slippered feet. She knew he wore slippers – they were placed neatly on the hearth waiting for him.

At her side was a small, round-topped table. On it was a brass ashtray with some pipe tappings in it, a vase of paper spills, and a pile of magazines. Idly she fingered them then she started up in surprise for on the cover of one at the top of the pile was a picture of herself complete with glossy lipstick, eyeshadow, mascara, her hair just slightly windswept. She flipped through the rest, one or two *Scottish Field*s, a farming journal, mainly women's magazines – more evidence of the female – or females in his life!

She stared at the photograph of herself – unless he was blind he must surely have seen it; he knew who she was – or rather, what she was, had probably known from the moment he set eyes on her. The thought dismayed her more than she would have thought possible. She had no earthly idea why – or did she? Was it because she didn't want him to see her as just a glamour girl? A pretty face in a magazine, a sophisticated town girl who knew little of country living?

I'm more than just a fashion model, Ullin MacBeth! her heart cried out, I'm flesh and blood as well. His words on the boat came back to her.

"You're from the town." Not a question, just a statement of fact which hadn't entirely been based on intuition. He had known all along what she did for a living and his manner towards her had made it quite plain that fashion model or not, to him she was just another tourist who was making quite a nuisance of herself one way and another.

Chapter Four

The opening of the outside door was barely heard by Chrisann but Mirk pricked up his ears and sat staring at the door, his tail thumping the rug.

Chrisann held her breath as footsteps came up the passage but it wasn't Ullin MacBeth who came in, it was a plump dark-haired girl whose pretty face was whipped to the colour of rosy red apples. As she caught sight of Chrisann she drew back slightly and said breathlessly, "Oh, I'm sorry, I didn' think Mr MacBeth had company. . . ." She paused and came further into the room, the wariness leaving her voice as she took a closer look at Chrisann and said laughingly, "I thought you were Claire Hamilton – just for a minute, in this dim light you looked like her."

Chrisann laughed too and introduced herself. "I'm Chrisann McNeil, I was camping on the other side of Ronnach but the wind blew my tent down and Mr MacBeth has gone to see if he can fix it."

The girl sat down opposite Chrisann. "Ach, you poor thing," she said sympathetically. "Dad was wondering how you would manage in this storm. Mum was all for sending Bob over to see how you were. I'm Mary Scott, I live in the house down by the jetty."

"Colin Mor's daughter?"

"Ay, the only one among two boys. They make my life a hell." Mary's burst of laughter belied the statement.

Her merry brown eyes swept over Chrisann approvingly. "I can see how my father was making such a fuss of you and why Mr MacBeth has gone out in this weather to fix your tent. If you don't mind me saying so you suit Kirsty's clothes, they might have been made for you. I was mad for a minute when I saw you wearing them. I thought you were that Claire Hamilton you see. She has a habit of helping herself to Kirsty's things. The poor girl gets hopping mad about it – but – I'm letting my tongue run away with me. Dad is always telling me to mind what I say but sometimes I forget."

Chrisann smiled faintly. In the space of a few minutes Mary had referred to two females who were obviously quite at home in Ullin MacBeth's house. "My own things were rather wet," she explained, "and Mr MacBeth told me to put on something dry."

Mary's dimples deepened. "Och, I'm sure Kirsty won't mind *you* wearing them. She's got a thing about Claire Hamilton though; she doesn't say much but it's there – under the surface – mind you, any woman would be jealous of Claire. She's the sort that attracts men – not that Mr MacBeth is the type to let any woman mess him around. I shouldn't say this, me getting married next Saturday, but I wouldn't mind his slippers under *my* bed for a night or two. He's so handsome and sexy all the girls go for him."

Chrisann wanted to ask a hundred questions but instead she bit her lip and said in a muffled voice, "Does Claire Hamilton live near here?"

"At Stonehurst over on Mull. She inherited the estate when her father died a year ago. It's a fine place but I doubt she has enough money to keep it going for much longer. That doesn't stop her from acting like a madam, riding about on her horse, looking down her nose at everyone. She means to keep Stonehurst and is out to marry a man who will know best how to manage the acres of farmland attached to the estate. That's why she's set her sights on Ullin, he's got a great knowledge of farming and he's got a good business head on his shoulders – and Claire knows he would love to get his hands on Stonehurst."

"I – I would have thought he would already be married," Chrisann said carelessly.

Mary's cheerful face took on the closed look Chrisann had seen on Colin Mor's. Mary stood up. "I must be going, I just came over with a pot of broth for Ullin's supper. I left it on the hall table." At the door she turned. "It was nice meeting you, Miss McNeil—"

"Please call me Chrisann."

"All right – Chrisann . . ." she hesitated. "I'm sorry I cut you off just now. The fact is well – you're a stranger and I've already said too much. I'll tell you this though, Mr MacBeth isn't married – not now – his wife is dead. He doesn't like to speak about it and I know you won't mention it – I feel you can be trusted even though I've only just met you – not like that Claire; Mum says she's a flighty one. . . ." She giggled. "There I go again, talking too much. I hope you get your tent fixed and get a dry bed for the night – if I know Mr MacBeth, he'll make sure of that."

Chrisann only just caught the muttered last words. A faint shock of unease shivered through her. Now that she was out of the unmerciful elements and was dry, warm and comfortable, her full powers of reasoning were returning. What on earth was she doing here? In the home of Ullin MacBeth? He was a complete stranger to her. What she knew of him and had heard about him weren't the sort of things to set her mind at ease. Mary had implied his fondness for the female sex. Chrisann shivered. Oh yes, she could well believe that as pictures flashed into her mind of Ullin MacBeth's handsome aloof features; those blue eyes of ice, lit with a raging inner fire as she had struggled with him out there in the passageway; that lithe, lean body, the animal warmth of it beating into her. The only contact had been through his hands gripping her wrists and though there had been pain she hadn't felt it as such. . . . So overwhelmed had she been by his masculine nearness . . .

She jumped as Mirk got to his feet and stood at the living-room door wagging his tail. It seemed as if Mary had only just left but Chrisann realized she hadn't noticed time as she had sat there at the fire thinking, her mind overwhelmed with thoughts of a man she barely knew.

A few minutes elapsed in which she guessed that Ullin MacBeth was removing his outdoor garments, then footsteps padded up the hall, soft as the tread of a tiger, and he came in to receive a rapturous welcome from Mirk. His fair hair was plastered over his forehead and raindrops glistened on his bronzed face. Chrisann was annoyed to feel her heart leaping wildly in her breast at sight of him. She had only met him yesterday yet he was wreaking emotions in her she had never experienced before.

His blue eyes were dark with anger and when he spoke his voice was tight. "Don't you know *anything* at all about camping?" he demanded furiously. "The main guys of your tent have snapped clean through and it's impossible to fix them tonight. Don't you know that they ought to be loosened off in wet weather? Don't you know even *that*?"

Chrisann reeled at the outburst. She fought down her nerves and answered coldly, "I forgot – I simply forgot. I was so cold and miserable last night I—"

"You forgot! Marvellous! I wonder why you bothered to try your hand at living in the great outdoors because it is very obvious you know nothing at all about it!"

"How dare you—"

"You'll have to stay here tonight," he interrupted, his voice clipped. "There's a room upstairs you can have—"

"I won't stay here to be insulted!" she stormed. "I'd rather spend the night in a barn than stay here and listen to you shouting your head off."

She stood up, tossing her head defiantly, her face pale with hurt and rage. His jaw tightened and he stood aside from the doorway, with a gracious sweep of his hand indicating that the way was free for her to go.

"Have it your own way." His tone was biting. "The night awaits you, complete with howling winds and torrential rain. No doubt Colin Mor and Jean would give you a bed for the night but as every space in their house is occupied it will not be easy. Oh, they are a mannerly family and it is likely that one of the boys would give up his bed to you – so – why don't you run along and ask?"

Chrisann fought a fierce and bitter battle with her pride but in the end she had to admit to herself that she was defeated and she said in a low voice, "I wouldn't dream of putting Colin Mor and his wife out on my behalf, they are much too nice. No – I think I would rather put you to some inconvenience and though I don't accept your offer graciously or willingly I see no other way out of my predicament – so – thank you, I will stay."

To her utter surprise he burst out laughing. "You have spirit," he grinned as he strode over to the hearth to push his feet into slippers. Crouched by the fire, his hands stretched out to the heat he went on, "If we are to spend some time under the same roof I suggest we call a truce and introduce ourselves. I'm Ullin Duncan MacBeth, you can call me Ullin – everyone does. I prefer to be informal."

She thought, You could have fooled me but she found herself warming to his change of mood and she smiled. "Ullin Duncan – that's rather cheeky, isn't it? History was never one of my best subjects but I seem to remember my teacher telling me that King MacBeth slew his predecessor King Duncan."

"Your memory serves you well. It was my father who bestowed me with my middle Christian name – he always did have a sense of humour."

"And Ullin? No relation to the Lord Ullin of Thomas Campbell's poem?"

He shrugged his broad shoulders. "My mother's doing, she was a romantic. I don't think there's any connection or she would have mentioned it."

He glanced towards her, his eyes deep pools in the shadows of firelight, and she was so overwhelmed by his nearness she got up and walked a little way from the fire, then she swung round on him. "I wonder, would you have been more willing to bring me over to Ronnach if I had quoted Campbell's poem to you?" Before he could reply she struck a dramatic pose and cried, "'A chieftain to the Highland's bound cries, "Boatman do not tarry! And I'll give you a silver pound to row us o'er the ferry. O, I'm the chief of Ulva's isle – and this Lord Ullin's daughter"'."

He didn't smile, instead he appraised her slim figure and glowing face and said slowly, "No, I might have thought you slightly mad and left you high and dry over on Mull – besides this is Ronnach, not Ulva. . . ." He paused then went on, "Never mind all that and what I said about your inexperience with country ways; despite it I would say that your stay on the islands is doing you some good. When I first saw you, you were too pale –

tonight you wear no make-up yet your cheeks bloom as bonny as those of any Highland lass."

Her face grew rosier still at his words and in confusion she turned away.

"You haven't told me your name yet." His voice held undertones of friendliness.

"Chrisann Thea McNeil."

"Thea?"

She spun round and laughed. "Yes, isn't it awful what parents do to their children? My mother has a favourite brother called Theadore. When I was born she couldn't very well give me that as a middle name so she had to make do with Thea."

"Couldn't she have waited and given it to a son instead?"

"I'm an only child. They waited a long time for me and knew there would be no more – so Chrisann Thea I am."

He got up and padded towards her to stand over her, so tall she felt swamped by him. "How very fortunate for the men in your life that you didn't turn out to be a Theadore."

She wanted to back away from him but stood on the spot as if held by a magnet. "What – I don't know what you mean."

"Oh, come now, don't act the little innocent. Surely you must have boyfriends – reams of them – a desirable girl like you is surely no stranger to the male sex."

A pang of unease shot through her and she stammered, "I – there's no one special."

"Oh, but there is someone then, someone who takes you in his arms and kisses you – like this."

His head came down and his lips brushed hers, warm and firm. It was a mere fleeting touch and over with instantly yet Chrisann was stunned. She felt the room spinning and her heart fluttering so fast she thought he must surely hear the pounding of it. Her legs trembled beneath her and she put out a hand to steady herself only to find that the only support to be had was in the restraining arm he had flung out as if he had meant to encircle her body in it. Briefly she let her hand remain where it was, against the hard steel of his muscles; felt the fire of his flesh searing through her. Quickly she drew away from him as if from the pain and danger of a furnace.

"I told you, I don't like to be formal," he drawled. He was filling her vision, totally consuming her strength with the power of his personality.

She backed away from him, finding refuge in a fresh upsurge of anger. "Is that so," she lashed out at him. "When first you spoke to me on Mull you were uncouth – and so ill-mannered you pretended on our second meeting not to recognize me – now you feel at liberty to take advantage of me and kiss me."

"Take advantage of you! You've been asking for it ever since I clapped eyes on you. You loved it and don't try to tell me otherwise." Ignoring her gasp of anger he went on coolly. "Remind me sometime to teach you what a real kiss is like – that was only for starters. As for me being bad-mannered back there – I felt you needed a lesson in manners yourself. You behaved like a spoiled brat when you didn't immediately get your own way about the ferry. You were rude, ungracious and positively ill-tempered. I knew at once you were a girl who was used to getting her own way and I decided to teach you a lesson. Folks on the islands don't take kindly to uppity strangers telling them what to do. We have a cure for bad-tempered brats here: a good spanking usually works wonders."

"Well, thank you very much!" she hissed, her nostrils aflare with indignation. "Were your notions about me intuitive or born of the fact that you knew only too well who I was – a city girl, a fashion model, a—"

"You grow more intriguing with every passing minute," he broke in roughly. "How the hell could I know who you were or what you did for a living?"

"This!" She flounced to the table and withdrew the magazine which sported her picture. Pushing it into his hand she cried, "Don't pretend with me, Ullin MacBeth! Of course you knew who I was; surely you must have seen that magazine with my photograph in it."

He stared at the cover picture for a long time before he looked at her quizzically.

"Well, well, forgive me. It would seem I'm in the presence of a successful career girl." Angrily he tossed the magazine onto the sofa. "What the hell do you take me for? A man who hasn't got anything better to do than sit there looking at women's magazines?"

"Sorry if I was mistaken," she said coldly. "You're right, these magazines are for women – and from what I see and hear there's plenty of evidence in *this* house of a woman's influence – or should I use the plural form as it would seem there are one or two queuing up to share your fire."

She immediately regretted the indiscretion. His eyes bored into her like twin steel drills; his jawline tightened. "And now I can add you to my score," he gritted. "You've only been here five minutes and think you know it all, eh? Well, I'm damned if you'll get much chance to ferret into my private affairs! I'll make it my business to see that your tent will be fixed and ready for you first thing tomorrow."

"Good." She meant to sound firm but her voice quavered miserably. She wanted to know who owned the pretty things in the bathroom, the clothes, who read the women's magazines, but the sting lash of his words made her only too aware that she had put her foot very firmly in it and the chances of getting to know Ullin MacBeth better were now very slim indeed.

He stomped into the hall only to return in seconds holding a large earthenware pot.

"Mary left that," Chrisann told him sullenly.

He grinned wryly. "I see – and Mary's tongue ran away with her as usual." He snapped on the overhead light and came over to stand by Chrisann, his keen eyes studying her face. "You look done in. Are you hungry?"

Chrisann hadn't given much thought to food since entering the home of Ullin MacBeth but now she was aware of her empty stomach and she nodded. "A little."

"A bowl of Jean's broth will soon see you right. I think there might be some cold chicken in the fridge. All right?"

"That sounds marvellous." She could hardly get the words out. His lips were very close to her face, his hair was a startling sheaf of pale gold under the electric light, she could see plainly the pulse beating strongly in his bronzed neck. His hand came out and he stroked her arm with an intimacy that made her shiver.

"Angora," he breathed softly. "There's something about angora over a woman's flesh that makes me . . ." He stopped and laughed. "Whatever it makes me, despite it you're shivering. I'll go and rustle up some food."

He went out and into a room across the hall and she thought, Did the owner of this sweater buy it to please you, Ullin MacBeth, because it makes you want . . . She wouldn't allow her thoughts to go on in that vein. Far better to enjoy this evening in this house with Ullin MacBeth. 'MacBeth' – the lively one. Oh yes, he was that all right. Alive, vibrant, domineering. She assumed he was one of the estate workers – yet the assumption didn't seem quite right to her. There was an enigmatic quality about him that set him apart but she would never get the chance to find out what it was. He had made it plain that he wanted to be rid of her as soon as it was possible.

He came back from the kitchen and they sat in the lamplight, eating soup, cold chicken legs, and bread and butter. Outside the rain hissed, the wind howled. Inside the clock ticked, Mirk snored, the fire crackled warmly. The hot soup glowed through her, bringing life back to her. Thanks to Colin Mor she had been able to have a bowl of cornflakes at lunchtime but that had been hours ago.

"Colin Mor saved my life this morning." Her words broke into the silence shrouding the room but she couldn't bring herself to meet the eyes of Ullin MacBeth. "I was led to believe that 'Mor' is the Gaelic for big or great – yet – he's quite a small man really."

"It's Colin's heart that earned him that name. I've known him and his family all my life and never known him refuse to do anyone a good turn."

She could feel his eyes on her and she felt her face burning. "I've seen you somewhere before," he sounded puzzled. "Oh, not in that girlie magazine, but I might have glimpsed you in Oban sometime." She glanced up quickly. He was making a cool, unhurried assessment of her, his eyes lingering on the round, enticing swell of her breasts. "Once seen never forgotten," he observed with a flash of the mocking smile she was beginning to know quite well and which never failed to infuriate her. "You wouldn't be any relation to James McNeil who owns the jeweller's shop in the High Street, would you?"

Chrisann didn't answer immediately. She was feeling nervous of him again and that in turn made her angry with herself. "James McNeil is my father," she said at last. "He and my uncle run the business between them."

"Small world. I used to pop into the shop occasionally. I might have seen you there." She shook her head. "Not very likely, I'm hardly ever home now, my job takes up most of my time . . ." She froze suddenly as a memory came to her of herself as a teenager helping her father to serve in the shop on a busy Saturday afternoon in summer. Through the mists of time she saw again an exquisitely dressed woman coming into the shop, hanging on to the arm of a tall, fair giant who walked with the firm sure tread of a tiger. Ullin MacBeth! No other! And from time to time, during the course of the busy years she had spent in London, a vision of that tall, unforgettable man had filtered into her mind, elusive, floating, dreamlike. And he remembered her too.

It had been years ago – would he remember the schoolgirl who had helped him to choose a piece of jewellery for the beautiful woman who accompanied him and whom he obviously adored? Had she been his wife? A woman who had filled his life – and who had died leaving him empty and unhappy. Mary had said he didn't like to speak about her. Did it hurt too much? Was this proud, dynamic, arrogant man capable of hurting that much?

His blue gaze was upon her, cold and disapproving. "You shouldn't allow your job to take up *that* much of your time," he told her curtly. "You ought to make a point of visiting your parents more often. God knows I'm no goody goody but I came home regularly to see my mother and father. They're gone now but I have memories of them I might never have had if I had stayed away."

Chrisann had always felt a certain measure of guilt at the way she had neglected her parents since her success in modelling and it was galling to be reminded of it by a man who had done nothing but rile her since they had first met.

"Lecture over?" she said shortly.

"Tetchy little brat." He was mocking her again, with his eyes and voice.

Briskly she changed the subject. "Will this rain last, do you think?"

"Tomorrow will be fine."

"How can you tell?"

"I was born on Mull. I know the ways of the weather. The storm will blow the clouds away; tomorrow the sun will shine."

"You sound so sure."

"As sure as I am that under that icy veneer of yours there is a creature of fire – just waiting for the right man to come along and kindle the smouldering passions you try so hard to hide."

She jumped to her feet. She had wanted the evening to last forever. She had wanted just to sit across from Ullin and observe his lithe body stretched out and relaxed like a sleepy cat. In her busy social life there had been numerous parties and functions but no matter how much glamour and glitter they had always left her feeling restless and discontented and sometimes, especially in the last year, bored. There was a sameness about them all, everyone trying too hard to be jolly, to laugh too loudly, to act rather than be themselves. Tonight had been so entrancingly different. In this house there was an atmosphere of peace. She and Ullin had indulged in spicy verbal battles but in between she had felt the peace, soothing her, washing into her – now – here he was again, deliberately tormenting her.

"You're a despicable beast!" she stormed. "You accuse me of nosing into your affairs when all you can do is make insulting personal remarks about me . . . and I'll tell you this, Ullin MacBeth, if you were the last man in the world I'd die rather than have anything to do with you."

"Is that so." He uncurled himself slowly and got to his feet. "We're alone in this house, Chrisann, we might be the only two people in the world – so how about putting your theories to the test?"

She felt frightened now and backed away. "Don't you dare touch me," she gasped. "Or I'll scream the place down."

He advanced slowly. "No one would hear you. We're on Ronnach, Chrisann, not in London. So, scream all you like – I don't think your protests will last very long."

She couldn't speak. She knew now why she was frightened. It wasn't of him, it was of herself, the treacherous weaknesses of her own body which had already betrayed her at the merest touch of his lips. "You're a hateful man, Mr MacBeth!" she lashed out. "Right from the beginning you've been hateful and with every passing moment I dislike you even more."

"Is that so," he taunted. "Well, I can see I'll have to do my very best to rectify that."

Roughly he pulled her into his arms and she found herself crushed against his lithe hard body. She struggled and tried to cry out but his lips were on hers, fiercely claiming her mouth, smothering her cries in a fiery kiss that melted away all her resistance. He pulled her in closer, moulding her body to his till she could feel the mounting passion in him. She was lost, lost, carried away, consumed by a fire of such intensity that the world spun away till it was swallowed up. And now it was just she and Ullin, locked in an intimate world of their own. Her body yielded to his and she gave herself up to an ecstasy she had never known existed between a man and woman.

She gave a soft little groan of pleasure and allowed her lips to respond willingly to his. She heard his quickening breath and the excitement mounted in her but quite suddenly he pushed her away. Dazedly she looked at him and saw in his eyes naked dark depths of violent desire.

"You respond pretty well to a man you hate," he said with a shaky laugh. "Just think what it would be like if you were just a wee bit fond of me. There would be no stopping you then. A model you might be in fashion but certainly not in your behaviour with strange men."

Chrisann felt herself shaking with reaction and humiliation. "Damn you! Damn you to hell!" she spat furiously. "You're the most despicable man I've ever had the misfortune to meet!"

"Time will tell," he grinned mockingly. "Now," he patted her bottom and propelled her out into the passageway, "up to bed like a good little girl."

He was talking to her as if she was a naughty schoolgirl. She wanted to run away, out of the house, to flee from him, but she knew she could never flee from her own feelings of humiliation and self-loathing – and besides – she had nowhere to run to. The wind was howling harder, the rain beating a tattoo against the windows.

"Where do I go?" she asked coldly.

"Second door on the right. I've laid out some night things for you – and of course you know where the bathroom is. I'll try not to disturb you in the morning. You'll find eggs and bacon in the fridge, help yourself. Colin Mor or one of the boys will get along over and fix your tent. By the way, I brought your bike up. It's in one of the sheds at the back."

"Thank you, you think of everything," she said woodenly and felt his eyes following her as she turned away. She stumbled upstairs, feeling breathless and unreal. Her heart was thudding in her breast, her body trembling.

The bedroom was very feminine and tasteful with a pink carpet covering the floor and a flowery duvet on the bed. The nightdress he had laid out for her was of oyster-coloured silk. She fingered the soft material as she looked round the room. One wall was taken up with white wardrobe units; on the opposite wall was a white dressing table on which was set cologne sprays and perfumes and an expensive brush and mirror set.

Who is she? Who is she? thought Chrisann in frustration. Claire Hamilton? The Kirsty Mary had mentioned but hadn't enlarged upon? Whoever she was, she was plainly indulged – and very much loved. Ullin MacBeth was obviously used to dealing with women. The way he had handled her hadn't been in the manner of a man who was woman-shy. He had been rough, firm, confident. He had expertly attended to her needs: clothed her; fed her; laid out exquisite nightwear, unerringly choosing the right things, the sort of things that would appeal to any fashion-conscious woman.

Chrisann went over to the wardrobes and rather guiltily looked into them, surprised to discover they were more than half-empty, containing enough garments a woman might need for a week – or a long weekend. Chrisann bit her lip. Was he that kind of man? The sort who enjoyed female companionship when the mood took him but otherwise remaining unfettered? Anger consumed her. What did she care? He wasn't to be trusted. There was something very strange about him. She had been right to feel about him as she did. If he had had his way she would have become just another of his passing fancies. She shivered in another burst of self-loathing. She had wanted him to kiss her, to go on kissing her, never to stop and it disgusted her to know she could desire such things from a complete stranger.

She slipped into the silken nightdress and slid under the duvet. He had even remembered to switch on the electric blanket. The bed was warm and soft. A feather bed. How lovely. The last time she had slept in a feather bed had been when she was a little girl on holiday at Aunt Jane's house in Nairn. She didn't want to sleep. All she wanted to do was to lie in that soft warm haven, hearing the wind keening outside, reliving every moment of the evening she had just spent with a stranger called Ullin – yes – even those moments that were almost beyond bearing to remember.

She could hear him moving about downstairs. Dishes rattled then a short while later she heard him calling on Mirk. A door shut softly, then there was silence. He was having a last smoke perhaps, sitting by the dying embers, Mirk's head on his feet. He might be thinking, thinking about tomorrow, the tasks that awaited him on the estate – or maybe he was thinking about the evening he had just spent with her. Impatiently she turned her head on the pillows. Of course he wasn't. Why should he? She was nothing to him, just a passing ship he had tried to manipulate according to his moody whims.

Yet – oddly – she felt secure in his house; secure and safe. Something tugged at her mind. She remembered again the sheer animal power of his body against hers. The feeling of security left her. She wouldn't sleep, not till she heard him come upstairs and go to his own room. She snuggled into the pillows to wait. They were soft, so soft, and she was so exhausted she felt drained. Her eyes closed and in seconds she was drifting into oblivion, drifting and dreaming.

Chapter Five

She was running, running over fields, splashing through ditches, jumping over frothing burns. Lightning crackled, thunder reverberated over the hills. All around there was terror, it beat into her, quickening her heart to a mad gallop. She wanted to stop running, to regain her breath but people were chasing her: Anthony Keats, Raymond Carstairs, dozens of photographers, hairdressers, make-up people. In the distance a golden chariot appeared driven by a Norse God wearing a helmet of palest gold. Then she saw it wasn't a helmet, it was hair the colour of ripe wheat, so bright it dazzled her and she saw eyes that sparkled like sapphires in the sun. Raising his whip he cracked it over the shoulders of the mob and they began running away, looking over their shoulders in awe. Chrisann stopped her demented flight and waited, half afraid, half wonderingly as the chariot stopped beside her and a voice said, "Come on, you're safe now. Take my hand."

She held out her hands and strong arms lifted her up. A great warmth was all around her, coursing through her flesh till it burned. The sapphire eyes were upon her, mesmerizing her, willing her to raise her face to his. Fiery lips seared over hers, passionate, demanding. The body of the Norse God was hard; she felt herself yielding to it. His hands were stroking her hair, her neck, her shoulders. Her breasts tautened and she waited for the touch that would send her into heaven. His hands were caressing the curves of her body and a little cry caught at the back of her throat.

"No, no, I mustn't let you do that, I mustn't . . ." Chrisann woke with a start, cutting short the sweet delirium of the dream. Her heart was racing madly and for a terrified moment she thought that Ullin MacBeth was there in the room beside her. Faint sounds came from downstairs and for a few dazed seconds she wondered if he hadn't yet come up to his room. But it was daylight, he was already up and starting his day . . . She ought to get up too but she was tired, so tired . . . She drifted into a deep and dreamless slumber.

It seemed just minutes later she awoke to hear the sound of feet beating a tattoo up the stairs. Before she could gather her senses the door burst open and Ullin MacBeth stood there. He was ruffled looking, his jaw was tense and his eyes were snapping with annoyance. In a few swift strides he reached the bed and stood glaring down at her.

"What is it?" she gasped. "You look—"

"On your way up here last night, did you leave a gate open?" he demanded harshly. Chrisann, still drugged with sleep, stared at him. Her mind raced, taking her over her mad dash for shelter the night before. There *had* been a gate, and on the other side of it sheep, hundreds of them.

"Yes, I think I did," she stammered. "I couldn't see where I was going. I—"

"You let all the damned sheep out!" he shouted at her, his face ablaze with temper. "All the animals that took all of yesterday for me and the men to round up ready for clipping and dipping today. It will take us a whole day to get them together again! Trouble! You've been nothing but trouble since you came here." He ran his fingers through his thick thatch and glared at her. She had reeled backwards onto the pillows at his outburst but now she sat up and glared back, her eyes a storm-cloud purple.

"I didn't intentionally let all your damned sheep out!" she blazed back at him. "I'm sorry about it but it was an accident! Most humans make mistakes from time to time but I can see you are such a high and mighty saint you always do the right things! Oh God, I hate you, Ullin MacBeth! I didn't like you from the first! You were rude, uncouth, a – a bully. And now, if you have a grain of human decency you'll get out of this room so that I can get dressed and leave this house at once!"

He bent down till his face was just inches from hers. There was a flush on his cheekbones, the pulse was beating swiftly in his neck, a muscle in his jaw was working. "I'll get out of this room in my own time," he grated. "Don't you tell me what to do in my own house."

His eyes travelled to the white cream of her neck and shoulders and she shivered as he coolly and silently appraised her body. The sun had risen quite high in the sky. A beam of it slanted through the window and poured over his towering figure. He was like a bronze giant in the searching rays, his muscles strained against his thin shirt. She could see the fuzz of hair covering his arms; they were like little threads of spun gold. They were both in a pool of golden warmth and – oh God! It was happening to her again. Her heart seemed to stop beating for a moment before it began to race madly. She felt powerless to move and lay quite still, her hair spread over the pillows like a cloud of night-black silk.

"Trouble you may be but you come in a very attractive form." His voice had changed, it was low and seemed to come from a very long way off. "I shouldn't have shouted at you like that. . . ." His change of mood put her off her guard. She felt unreal, as if she was back once more in a dream world. His hand came out to stroke her hair then his mouth came down on hers, hard and demanding. The touch of his hands on her bare shoulders made her tremble; his kiss was of fire, deep, searing, sending warmth through every fibre of her being. With a little cry she responded to him wildly. His fingers traced a trail of red-hot fire down her spine till she tingled with longing and her arms came up to wind themselves round his hard, rippling shoulders. His lips were pushing hers apart and she offered no resistance but drew him even closer as quivers of rapture spread through her, consuming her, and she was yielding to him, moulding the soft contours of her body to his hard, burning flesh.

Naked desire, such as she had never before experienced, surged in every vein in her body and she was swept away in a tide of sensual arousal. It was as if her body was being awakened for the first time and there was simply no way she could control it – she wanted to give herself – willingly – wantonly . . . Suddenly she stiffened . . . this room – this bed – how many women had lain in it? Given themselves willingly to this virile, demanding man? This man called Ullin? Ice cold fear doused the fire in her veins and she began to struggle out of his grasp, her breath catching raggedly in her throat.

He released her and straightened up to look down on her. His eyes were faraway and he was breathing hard but his voice when he spoke was brusque. "The old game, eh? Playing hard to get when your body is screaming out for more. You're not the frozen little miss you try very hard to make out to be. Last night and just now has proved that you're a fireball under that cool exterior. You shouldn't play with fire, Chrisann, you really shouldn't, because one day you'll end up getting burnt. A man can take only so much teasing and I'm very much flesh and blood – so be warned, my girl. If it hadn't been for the fact that Kirsty is waiting for me outside I would have taken you just now – and you would have let me because you want me very much whether your puritan little mind likes the idea or not."

"You – you conceited pig," she gasped weakly. "The only thing I want at this moment is to see you out of my sight."

"You've got it," he said curtly, striding to the door and banging it viciously behind him.

Chrisann lay back against the pillows, drained of strength, very aware of her swiftly beating heart, and of a great sense of humiliation that made her feel cheap and degraded. Never, never again would she so much as touch Ullin MacBeth. The very sight of the man was enough to send reason out of the window. He only had to look at her to set her senses reeling. Yet she despised him utterly; he was boorish, arrogant and conceited beyond measure. A man like that could never love a woman for herself, he was motivated only by pure physical desire and she would take very great care never to allow herself to become another of his conquests.

Kirsty . . . he had said she was waiting outside. Chrisann leapt out of bed and went over to the window. There, on the sun-bathed drive was Ullin and clinging to his arm was a stunning looking girl with long blonde hair and a neat figure clad in tight jeans and a blue cotton blouse.

Chrisann cowered back behind the curtains as the girl's voice floated clearly. "Darling, what have you been doing all this time? I've just arrived and already you're neglecting me."

Hating herself Chrisann was compelled against her will to take another peep at the scene below. Ullin's arm was round the girl's waist. She was snuggling into him while round them frisked two sheepdogs. They began to walk towards a truck parked a little way off. Chrisann's heart quivered then once more began to race madly. She knew without question that it was Kirsty's toiletries which filled the bathroom; that it was Kirsty's bed she had slept in; that it was Kirsty's things she had worn. But she was so young – young and desirable to a man like Ullin.

A curlew was bubbling out its heart in the sun-bathed world outside but Chrisann barely heard it. She would get out of this house just as quickly as she could and see to it that she wouldn't give that arrogant brute the opportunity to catch her off guard again.

Shakily she made her way to the bathroom to wash. On the shelf above the washbasin a tube of toothpaste lay capless and a wry smile lifted her mouth. Even the most thorough of people could lapse enough to leave traces of untidiness. Mechanically she screwed the cap back on then, having washed, she turned to the bath to see if her clothes were dry enough to wear. But they weren't there and she made her way down to the living-room. As she had guessed, her clothes were there, neatly spread over the airer which stood a safe distance from the fireplace. A shiver ran through her; he was attentive, meticulous – but how he spoiled all that with his self-confident arrogance.

Feeling utterly miserable she dressed and wandered into the sun-flooded kitchen. Everything was neat and suprisingly well equipped with the latest electrical gadgets. Surely above all else he wasn't an extraordinary cook too. But of course not. He was the sort of man that had women at his beck and call. Jean probably mothered him as far as he would allow; Mary ran to his house in ghastly weather with pans of home-made broth; as for his lovers – he probably only picked those who excelled themselves in the kitchen as well as the bedroom. She smiled. To think of it in that light took some of the sting away. He was welcome to Claire and Kirsty and they were welcome to him. She loathed herself for having had so little resistance against his persuasive animal magnetism and she loathed him for making her feel little better than a man-hungry Jezebel.

She started at the sound of wheels crunching on gravel and her heart raced into her throat. Not *him* again, she thought wildly. She had barely recovered from their last encounter.

The kitchen door flew open letting in a flood of sunshine. The girl called Kirsty stood there while two cats wound themselves round her legs and several hens marched inside to peck at crumbs on the floor.

Chrisann was minded afresh that she was on a Hebridean island called Ronnach and how different it all was to what she was used to.

The girl flashed Chrisann a friendly smile and coming into the kitchen filled the kettle and put it on the stove. While she was busily clattering with the teapot she chatted easily. "I came back to make up some flasks of tea for myself and Dad," she explained casually. "Actually Jean gave us plenty to take away with us but Claire has just arrived to help with the sheep so I slipped away for a while."

Chrisann couldn't follow any of this and the girl laughed and held out her hand. "Sorry, I should have introduced myself. I'm Kirsty MacBeth. I'm on holiday from college and I'm staying over at Strathullin on Mull but I decided to slip over early this morning and give Dad a hand here. He didn't mind that too much but when Claire arrived just now he got a bit uptight though normally he likes having her around – it's just . . ." Kirsty's friendly smile flashed out again, "Dad sees Ronnach as a kind of escape and hates to be followed around when he's here."

Only certain facets of the conversation pierced Chrisann's mind, the most startling being that this girl was Ullin's daughter. She stammered, "Then – it's your things I've made use of, your bed I've slept in. . . ."

Kirsty pushed back her mane of hair and the blue eyes that smiled at Chrisann were Ullin's. "Think nothing of it," she said pleasantly. "Mind you, I wouldn't say that to anyone – that Claire for instance – oh, never mind her just now! Actually, since Dad told me you were here I've been dying to meet you. I devour fashion articles and I've seen you so many times on paper I felt I knew you even before I met you. I love the things you model, I adore studying patterns and textures."

She went on to tell Chrisann that she was studying textiles at a college in the Borders, that she enjoyed fishing, riding, swimming and cooking in her spare time. "When it came to choosing my career it was a toss up between Cordon Bleu cookery and textiles," she ended enthusiastically. Pouring the tea into flasks she then went to pour milk into saucers for the cats.

Chrisann suddenly felt very hungry. She couldn't begin to understand why she felt a strange joy surging through her heart but it was flipping as gaily as the big double-yoked eggs she was soon tossing in the pan. Kirsty had agreed to join her in a feast of ham and eggs and crunchy toast and soon they were sitting companionably at the table. It was lovely sitting in the peaceful kitchen with the cats lapping and the hens pouncing on crumbs. Chrisann closed her eyes. How wonderful it was, how different from anything she had ever known. All that she had thought real was a million miles away. This was her reality, the sweet fragrance of grass filling the air, the sleepy clucking of the hens . . . a raucous bellow made her jump and Kirsty laughed. A large sheep was peering into the kitchen, its strange yellow eyes full of curiosity.

Kirsty rose with agility and grabbing a broom chased the hens from the kitchen and with a bit of firm persuasion the ewe finally went also. Kirsty picked up the flasks and went to the door. "I'd better rush," she said then added with a smile, "on the other hand it won't do Claire any harm to wait a bit. *I* for one don't jump when she snaps her fingers. Just the same I'd better go. The men went off round the hill leaving Dad with Claire."

"Is – she nice?" Chrisann asked casually.

"In nature or looks?"

"Well – both, I suppose."

"She knows where she wants to go and pity help anything or anyone who stands in her way. She can be utterly charming on one hand and on the other harder than flint. She's beautiful and she knows it, the sort men do handstands for, and the sort other women hate."

"Why should they?"

Kirsty's blue eyes gleamed. "She could get any man she wants. One wiggle of those sexy hips of hers and even the old crofters' eyes are sparkling."

"Then – why hasn't she married?"

"Because she's been biding her time. Claire doesn't want just any man, she wants to marry into wealth and position, and she's got her claws well and truly into Dad." Kirsty sounded rather bitter and in a welter of confusion Chrisann stared at her. Kirsty saw the look and she shook her blonde head. "Sorry Chrisann, I assumed you knew who Dad was. I'll tell you later, I don't have time to explain now." At the door she turned. "I'm spending a few days here to help out with the dipping. We won't get through it all today. Why don't you have the guest room along the corridor? It's small but adequate and it would be nice to have a real good chin-wag with you . . . what's the matter? You're blushing."

"In my mad dash through the storm last night it was me who let all the sheep out," explained Chrisann guiltily.

"Stop worrying. Claire might make some capital out of it but no one else will . . . but that doesn't answer my question. Will you stay here tonight?"

Chrisann was about to say yes but a picture of Ullin's mocking eyes flashed into her mind. He would see an abandoning of camp as an admission of her inexperience of outdoor life and she certainly wasn't going to give him that satisfaction.

"I'd better not, Kirsty, I believe my tent will be fixed by now."

"Oh well, if you change your mind. . . ."

Kirsty was about to dash off but Chrisann called after her, "Kirsty, is it all right if I use your phone?"

"Help yourself," cried Kirsty over her shoulder. The next minute the truck rattled away and Chrisann went into the hall and dialled her home number. It was her mother who answered.

"Hallo, Mum," said Chrisann. "I thought I would give you a ring and let you know I survived the storm."

"Chrisann, how lovely to hear you," Mrs McNeil's voice was full of relief. "Dad and I were worried. Where are you?"

"On Ronnach – in a house here – my tent blew down last night."

"What house?"

"Ullin MacBeth's house. I think he's one of the estate workers – at least I did," she added faintly as she recalled some of Kirsty's words.

"Ullin MacBeth!"

"Yes, do you know him?"

"I should think everyone knows *of* him. He comes into Dad's shop occasionally and of course he's the biggest landowner on Mull *and* he owns Ronnach. He inherited it all when his elder brother died a couple of years ago. There was a lot of tragedy in the family I believe but from what I hear Ullin is a very go-ahead man. With the help of the Highland and Islands development board he's built a fair number of holiday chalets on pockets of his land that weren't of good grazing value. I understand he's done the same with some land in Angus but he has another smallish estate in Invernesshire where he likes to go in the shooting season. . . ."

"Oh well, what's one more estate anyway?" quavered Chrisann weakly.

"Chrisann, didn't you know any of this?"

"I'm finding out fast, just put my ignorance down to the fact I've spent most of the last nine years in London. Listen Mum, I'll have to go, I just wanted to let you know I'm safe. Are you and Dad all right?"

"Fine, dear, hoping you'll manage a few days with us. Chrisann, has something happened? When you came on the phone you sounded – well different – happier somehow."

"Is that so unusual?

"Well, dear, you can be snappy sometimes and just lately you seemed always to be moody about something or other – but now . . ."

Chrisann forced a laugh. "It's Ronnach – so lovely and peaceful, I needed the rest. It will be business as usual next week but I'll try and get a couple of days with you and Dad first. I must go now, bye Mum, take care."

With a trembling hand she laid the phone carefully back in its cradle and stood leaning against the wall. What a fool she'd been! What a fool she'd made of herself! She had taken Ullin to be a farmhand, at best an estate worker – and all along it was he who owned Ronnach and other estates all over Scotland. No wonder she had sensed that he was different. That was putting it mildly.

He was rich, powerful, and obviously a hard-headed unsentimental business man who thought nothing of furthering his bank balance by building holiday accommodation on large chunks of his land. And he had the cheek to look down his nose at tourists! He had done it with her when she was nothing but a mere stranger to him. She shivered. What made her think she was anything more than a stranger to him now? He had done nothing but make a fool out of her from the moment she met him. He had deluded her into thinking he was something he wasn't. She supposed it gave him great satisfaction to put on an act like that. How he must have sniggered up his sleeve at so successfully taking her in.

He was a despicable creature – yet – why did her heart twist with longing at the remembrance of the intimacies that had passed between them? Even the very thought of his lips pressed against hers as they had been that morning, sent pangs of hungry desire trembling through her and she felt humiliated beyond measure to know that she should feel such physical urges for a man who was nothing more than an expert womanizer and a calculating one at that, ready to pounce at any available opportunity. Mary had said that he wanted to get his hands on Stonehurst; at the time Chrisann had taken it to mean that it was his ambition to marry a woman who would carry him further up the ladder, that the lands attached to Stonehurst would be just the thing a go-ahead farmer could make use of but now she thought differently. He probably wanted to develop it all, stick holiday houses on every available patch. If he married Claire he would get his hands on it all and bend her to his way of thinking. From the sound of it she wouldn't need much persuasion.

She wanted wealth, Ullin wanted land, it was as simple as that. . . . Chrisann pressed her fist to her mouth as if to push back the feeling of resentment that had sprung up in her at the very idea of Claire Hamilton, a woman who was, as yet, just a name to her.

With a resolute shrug she went outside. It was a glorious day. Soft cirrus clouds sailed over the majestic blue dome of the heavens. The air was warm, heavy with the perfumes of a variety of wild flowers. The bleating of the ewes and lambs echoed from the hills; shaggy coated Highland cows grazed peacefully on the machair. They did not look up as Chrisann passed by and all at once she wasn't afraid of them any more, not even of a big bull who was even more placid-looking than the cows.

She found her tent efficiently fixed and over the sun-warmed rocks she placed bedding and clothing to dry. Her jeans and a pink T-shirt were reasonably dry and going behind a rock she changed into them.

The ruins of the crofting hamlet were on the northern side of Ronnach and to these she made her way. She found them on the shoreline, roofless, tumbledown, yet without the gauntness of larger ruined dwellings. Harebells and thyme grew among the grass inside the grey shells. In one a great solid chimney-breast stood intact on an end wall, the blackened fireplace full of rubble and roots of bushes. She ran her hands over the stonework and a great sadness overwhelmed her. There was an atmosphere here that was spiritual.

Echoes of the past were all around. She could picture the family that had once lived here, imagine them gathered round the fire in the cold nights of winter, the old ones to recount the tales that had been passed down from generation to generation. She could almost hear their lilting voices, see the hands of the womenfolk busily spinning, weaving, knitting. In her mind she pictured the faces brushed golden by firelight, serene contented faces. How awful that they had been forced to leave such a tranquil way of life. She could hardly bear to think of them being herded into the boats that had carried them over the sea to foreign lands, exiled forever from their native Scotland.

She took a deep trembling breath and looked up at the sky. The sigh of the sea came to her, a sigh as of voices from the past. She wandered through all the houses. Some were huddled together, others set apart, but in every one she sensed life, not death. She gazed out of a crumbling window aperture towards Mull and saw blue shadows drifting lazily over the hills. Dimly she was aware of whistles and shouts on the road above her together with the bleating of sheep. Outside the cottage a stone rolled and she leapt back from the window, her heart racing. Ullin came through the doorway, stooping low to avoid the lintel.

"Thought I would find you in one of these." He studied her face and she felt it flushing a fiery pink. "You look wistful. Are you?"

Keeping her distance she said, "A little. I feel so much of what it must have been like for the folk who lived here."

He looked at her approvingly. "I know how you feel. I often come here myself when I need to get things into perspective."

She felt overpowered by his presence. He was devastatingly handsome in a blue open-necked shirt that showed to advantage his bronzed skin. She mustn't allow him to come near her, to touch her. She was afraid of these equable exchanges that were effectively quelling the anger she had felt against him that morning. She felt an almost irresistible longing to lie once more in his arms, to run her fingers through his sun-bleached hair. . . .

"I'm sure you do," she said bitingly. "When you are king of all you survey it must make quite a change to taste humble pie now and again."

She could have bitten out her tongue. His unleashed anger cut across her like a whiplash as he demanded harshly, "What the hell is that supposed to mean?"

"It means that I know all about you, Ullin MacBeth!" she cried defensively. "I suppose you thought it was very funny, leading me to think that you were one of the estate workers when all the time you own it all. But I shouldn't really complain, I should thank you very humbly for allowing me to camp on your land. After all, I might have disturbed your sheep."

His eyes were blue ice in his blazing face. "Oh, you managed that quite successfully in the long run," he threw at her harshly. "And yes, indeed you should thank me for allowing you to camp. I don't normally allow tourists on Ronnach. You should think yourself very privileged."

"Privileged!" she cried in an outrage. "A privileged fool! You were right when you called me stupid last night. I was stupid to be taken in by you, to even think that you had any kind of humanity in you. How you must have laughed when I came running to you for help! You thought it proved I couldn't stand living in the wilds after life in the city—"

"And didn't it?" he cut in sarcastically.

"I can assure you it won't happen again," she raced on. "You saw me only as someone to amuse yourself with – a bit of a diversion on a rainy night. I suppose it gave you a great kick to pretend you were one of the workers. . . ."

"I did not pretend," he said coldly, "you assumed. You came to my house and although you tried to ferret things out of Mary you didn't ferret successfully enough so you assumed the rest. Why don't you admit that you were assumptive?"

"You're right, I was," she admitted miserably. "But you gave me every reason to think that you were anything but a wealthy landowner."

His eyes were boring into her and she couldn't face looking into them as he went on in a voice of steel, "If it's any of your business, Ronnach is my escape – somewhere to go when I feel the need to get away from responsibilities. I enjoy working side by side with the men, to feel I am one of them and not just some God Almighty laird ruling in a high-handed fashion from my castle. I never wanted any of it but when Gordon, my elder brother, died two years ago, I got it and I mean to make the most of it though I hardly need to explain any of this to you – though I must say you were correct when you said you created a diversion last night. It isn't every evening a beautiful girl knocks at my door and falls willingly into my arms – and you were willing, Chrisann; like it or not that lovely sexy body of yours can't help responding under the persuasion of a few kisses."

The mocking amusement was back in his eyes. Chrisann's cheeks burned, the pupils of her eyes were black with anger and humiliation. She felt her legs trembling. She couldn't withstand the sheer arrogance of this blond brute who seemed to take a joy in making her feel degraded at every turn. He came a step closer and she glanced up to see his eyes travelling slowly over her body, lingering on every curve with deliberate assessment, a gleam of devilish enjoyment in his gaze. He reached out and ran his strong brown fingers over her bare arm and she hated herself for the surge of longing that shot through her at his touch. He sighed and said conversationally, "Really, Chrisann, you want me to kiss you again, don't you? You want it very much."

"Take your hands off me," she stammered warningly while she fought to keep her breath even. "This morning you had me at a disadvantage but now I'm very much in control of myself."

"Really?" he enquired sardonically. "So you are admitting that you weren't in control this morning, that even while you were fighting me you wanted me with every shred of passion in your body and now we have all this fighting talk about self-control. I think I'll have to persuade you to prove that statement. You are at this moment fighting with yourself, your mind is desperately telling your body that you want nothing to do with me but your body won't obey the weak signals from your mind. That's true, isn't it, Chrisann?"

She backed away from him. "Leave me alone, Ullin, I will admit to no such ridiculous untruth."

"Stop behaving like a silly schoolgirl," he said smoothly. "If I took you in my arms this very moment you wouldn't be able to stop yourself catching fire, would you? You're not in bed now but that makes no difference. You want me to take advantage of you no matter where it is."

"Go to hell!" she yelled as panic mounted in her breast. "You take some beating for arrogance. I've met conceited men before but never one as hateful as you."

"Chrisann, I can see I'm wasting my breath; I'll have to prove my point to you," he said patiently.

His hand shot out to grip her arm with such brutal force she felt her flesh burning yet even while she cried out in pain she was so mesmerized by his virile power she felt unable to tear her eyes from his. She saw fire diffusing and melting the blue ice and with a strangled sob she made a clumsy attempt to get away from him. Her foot caught on a stone and he pulled her up and spun her round so that she stumbled into his arms.

"Obliging, aren't you?" he laughed mockingly then his head came down and his lips claimed hers in a kiss of such savagery she gave a little moan of terror. His arms were locked tightly round her, imprisoning her against his body with such force she couldn't struggle. But very soon she didn't want to. All she wanted was to lie in his arms and become not only his prisoner but his slave, to give him anything he asked of her.

She forgot how much she hated him, forgot her resolve never to respond to him again; instead she gave herself up to the sweet delirium of being kissed by him, to the wonderful excitement of feeling his lips pushing hers apart and his tongue probing into the warm, secret recesses of her mouth. He was no longer forcing her to bend to him, instead she was pressing herself closer and closer to his supremely hard-muscled body. The animal heat of him scorched through her thin top and she was conscious of a dizzy sensation of erotic desire tingling inside her, the likes of which she had never experienced before.

She became aware of his mounting arousal and the last shreds of her reason whirled away. She clasped her arms around his firm broad shoulders, her fingers playing with the strands of hair at the nape of his neck. From somewhere close by a blackbird trilled out a song and the sweetness and joy of it struck a chord deep in Chrisann's swiftly beating heart. . . .

A little breeze made her shiver suddenly as Ullin pushed her out of his warm embrace. His voice was low with amusement as he said, "I was only too right about you, Chrisann, and if you don't admit it I will be forced to repeat the performance all over again."

Though the sun beat down warmly she felt suddenly icy cold. "You think yourself very smart, don't you?" she said huskily. "It amuses you to experiment with people's emotions, it inflates that already over-inflated ego of yours. Was that how you treated your wife? Always trying to prove what a big man you were! Did you ever relent and tell her you loved her or did she go to her grave a lonely, rejected woman . . . ?"

The black fury in his eyes made her recoil. With a swift movement his hand flashed out to take her arm once more in a vice like grip. "Don't you ever speak to me about things you know nothing about!" he spat out harshly. "Do you hear?"

"You're hurting my arm, let me go," she begged with a muffled sob of fear. "I'm sorry I spoke about your wife. You're right, I know nothing about her but – but you're so cruel. You bring out the worst in people. You came down here and deliberately shattered my peace of mind. What do you expect me to do? Go down on my knees to you?"

"Oh no, not that," his voice was ominously quiet. "I just want you to face facts about yourself, one of them being that you've been fascinated by me ever since you first clapped eyes on me. You've wanted me to make love to you—"

"I don't, you forced yourself on me. I hate you and all your bullying ways—"

"You've made your feelings for me quite plain," he clipped. "But that doesn't stop your body crying out for fulfilment. I've proved that more than once; I've held you and felt the fire in you – so admit that I'm right."

"Is that what you came down here for?" she gasped. "To try and prove a ridiculous point?"

His blue eyes flashed. "No, I came to tell you that Jean has invited you to have lunch at her house but I thought I might kill two birds with one stone as the saying goes – so I'm not leaving till you tell me that I could overcome your so-called resistance any time I choose."

"Damn you – I won't do any such thing," she responded weakly.

"Oh well." His long limbs stirred into action and she

was reminded afresh of a loose-limbed tiger as he sprung into her path, effectively blocking her way of escape. "I can see I'll have to force you into an admission though I would rather it came from you voluntarily."

"All right," she whispered in desperation. "I think you might be able to—"

"Might? That's not good enough." He took another threatening step closer.

"Yes, yes," she said quickly. "You very likely could. Damn you to hell! It's likely that you could do anything you want with anybody you choose to victimize. Are you satisfied now? Or do you want blood?"

"No, that will do to be going on with." His lips lifted into a smile. "You know, Chrisann, it's worthwhile making you angry because your eyes grow really dark. They remind me of the little purple flower of the Crowberry which is the badge of my clan. It's a heathery-looking shrub and grows only on the wild slopes of moor and mountain. If you're very very nice to me and stop throwing those tiring temper tantrums I'll fetch you a bit from the moors."

She wanted to make a derisive retort but couldn't. He was standing so near she could see the pulse beating in his bronzed neck and in a welter of confusion she knew, that despite her hatred of him, she wanted once more to be held captive in his arms, to be kissed and kissed by that firm, persuasive mouth which was just inches away from her face. He saw the expression in her eyes and with a mocking laugh he stepped back and sat down on a nearby boulder.

The next moment she wondered if he had made the move away from her because he had heard footsteps approaching. She had been aware of nothing but his overwhelming presence but now she saw a movement at the door of the ruined cottage and spearing through her confusion she saw a pair of glittering amber eyes regarding her with cool disdain.

"Ullin, darling," the newcomer's voice drawled carelessly. "I thought I saw you coming down here. What on earth are you doing?"

She came through the doorway, a tall, slender, chestnut-haired beauty and Chrisann knew that she was face to face with Claire Hamilton, the girl who, till that moment, had only been a name to her.

Chapter Six

Everything about Claire was dazzling, from her gleaming sun-burnished chestnut hair to her long, smooth sun-tanned limbs. She was wearing a pale green figure-hugging top and white shorts which accentuated her brown shapely legs. Chrisann felt all at once very conscious of her pale skin and the streaks of dirt on her jeans from her rambles through the old crofthouses.

Ullin made the introductions and Claire's eyes flicked over Chrisann with unconcealed hostility. "Well, well," she observed laconically. "Little Bo-Peep in person." She gave a light little laugh of derision and walked over to Ullin to wind her arms possessively round his neck. "Come on, darling, you can't sit here all day," she smiled, intimately running her fingers over the top of his spine. "We have all those sheep to catch, and they certainly won't come running home on their own."

The sarcastic implications brought fire to Chrisann's cheeks. She clenched her fists at her sides and holding her head high she marched outside and began to climb up the terraced hill to the road where a moving sea of sheep were being kept together by three sheepdogs who in turn were obeying the commands and whistles of several men. Ullin strode past Chrisann to join the men and she found Claire at her elbow, her voice nonchalant as she said, "So, you're the maiden Ullin rescued from the storm last night."

"That's putting it in rather a melodramatic way," retorted Chrisann. "I prefer to think I went to him for help and he gave it."

"Indeed, he would," Claire sounded thoughtful. "I believe you stayed the night at Dykehill."

"Dykehill?"

"Yes, Ullin's hideaway, it's called Dykehill. He adores the place but while I find it rather romantic now and then I prefer my evenings with him at Strathullin House on Mull. Of course you haven't been there yet and as I believe your stay here is to be a short one you won't have the time to see very much of the place."

"Oh, but I'm beginning to enjoy myself," said Chrisann quickly, feeling an imperative urge to wipe the superior look from Claire's lovely, self-assured face.

"Really, oh well, from what I hear you'll be spending the rest of your stay under canvas."

Chrisann couldn't stop herself from saying, "Not necessarily, Kirsty has invited me to use the guest room at Dykehill."

Claire remained infuriatingly unperturbed. "Then, unlike last night, you won't be all on your lonesome. You are brave, a town girl spending the night alone in a remote country house."

"What do you mean?" Chrisann faltered.

"Why, didn't you know? Oh, my dear girl, I *am* sorry, I thought Ullin must have mentioned the fact that he spent the night at Sam's. Sam is one of the shepherds and as he isn't married Ullin's arrival late last night didn't cause him any inconvenience."

Chrisann suddenly remembered the sounds she had heard whilst lying in bed last night – Ullin's voice softly calling on Mirk, the quiet closing of a door. She had imagined he was letting the dog out for a last run before bedtime but instead he had sneaked away leaving her to spend the night alone in an empty house. How petty and childish. Had he thought she might wander up in the night and attack him!

She determined she wouldn't mention to him that she had found him out but feeling that she had to make some sort of stand in front of Claire she said as carelessly as she could, "How odd of him to do such a thing. Are you quite certain that a man of Mr MacBeth's obvious self-assurance would go scuttling away from his own house just because he had a strange woman under his roof? I heard him moving about in the kitchen this morning."

"He returned for some necessities," said Claire, flicking a speck of dust from her shorts and gazing towards the road as if Chrisann was boring her. "And Ullin didn't scuttle away as you put it; even if you haven't, he has his reputation to think about and won't allow anything silly to jeopardize it."

With that she ran to link her arm through Ullin's leaving Chrisann feeling miserably degraded. Kirsty came swishing through the grass, her fair hair blowing in the breeze. She looked at Chrisann's flaming cheeks and as they walked along together she observed sympathetically, "I see Claire's been getting at you. It's difficult as I know only too well but try not to mind too much. She's always got her claws out when Dad's on the scene."

She glanced at her father some distance in front, his bronzed rugged face relaxed into lines of tolerance as Claire spoke to him in a low voice. "He never seems to get angry with her," Kirsty sounded puzzled. "Yet he can with me. The trouble is she's so infuriatingly good at everything. You wouldn't think it to look at her but she can muck in as good as any man when it comes to things like sheep and cows – *and* she's a wizard with horses. . . ." Broodingly she watched as Claire slid her arm round Ullin's waist. "First it was Uncle Gordon; they were about to be married when he died very suddenly but for Claire the trail didn't stop there. Now it's Dad; as I told you she's got her hooks into him and the awful thing is I really do believe she's in love with him as well as his money. In a way I can understand, what woman could resist a man like that?"

Chrisann nodded and said unthinkingly, "When I first saw you I thought you were one of his harem, I never dreamed for one moment you were his daughter. . . ." She checked herself, afraid that she might have offended Kirsty but the girl's eyes sparkled with appreciation and she nodded.

"I know, he's so handsome and hardly looks thirty-seven. He was only twenty when I was born. I suppose it was one of those very swift passionate affairs that led too quickly to marriage. They made each other very unhappy. . . ." her blue eyes became faraway. "I can remember Mother nagging a lot, though in between there were times when they seemed to absolutely adore one another. The trouble was that Dad liked the country while Mother loved the bright lights. Before her marriage she lived in the city but Dad's work took him to the country and she wouldn't meet him half-way. . . ." Kirsty grew quiet for a few moments then she turned her quizzical blue gaze on Chrisann who was inwardly squirming as she remembered her unthinking words to Ullin about his wife.

"Did anyone tell you how she died?" asked Kirsty bluntly.

Chrisann shook her head, an anticipatory dread in her for she sensed from Kirsty's attitude that there had been dark tragedy in the MacBeth family though she was poorly prepared for Kirsty's next words.

"We came to live with Grandpa and Uncle Gordon

after Grannie died but Grandpa never quite got over her death and died soon after. Dad stayed to help Uncle Gordon deal with things. Mother hated being stuck in the country all the time. She went wild and was always throwing parties and doing anything she could think of for kicks. One day she bought a sports car; it was red, I can see it now, sitting in the driveway, sleek and gleaming. Uncle Gordon adored cars of all sorts. Mother was in a very abandoned mood that day, I remember it all plainly because I was home from school for the holidays. Mother and Uncle Gordon jumped into the car and roared away. She was driving, much too fast for the island roads. The car went over the cliffs at Calgary and rolled into the sea and they were both drowned. Dad, of course, inherited everything and he's worked really hard at it, though I know he often longs for the more ordinary kind of life we used to have."

In an effort to lead the conversation away from the appalling tragedy that had happened in the MacBeth family, Chrisann asked quietly, "Where did you live before?"

"Oh, all over the place. Dad came out well from agricultural college and managed land in various places. We even had a spell in New Zealand at one point, though Mother didn't like it there as all her friends were in Britain so we came back. She was happy for a while till we came here. Oh, it was glorious, paradise for Dad and me, but hell for Mother. You know, Chrisann, I believe that Claire thinks the MacBeth family owe her something because Uncle Gordon was taken from her just as she was about to marry into it all."

Chrisann glanced up and saw Ullin's bright head thrown back with amusement at something Claire had said. He laughed with Claire yet when he was with her all he ever did was torment her in every way possible.

A curly-haired boy of about five, was clinging to Ullin's free hand and to change the subject Chrisann asked Kirsty who he was.

"Oh, that's Jamie, Jean and Colin's grandson."

"I met Mary but she never mentioned she had a married sister."

"She hasn't," said Kirsty rather sadly. "Morag died giving birth to Jamie. It was one of those things. Poor Morag fell in love with a boy who wanted nothing to do with her when he found she was expecting a baby. Colin and Jean adore the wee boy and have brought him up as their very own."

"How very very sad," said Chrisann biting her lip. Her mind was reeling with all the things told to her by Kirsty and as they were nearing the fanks she made her excuses and walked away over the sunlit fields to the whitewashed house by the jetty. Jean welcomed her with reserve. She had light brown hair, blue eyes and a rosy fair complexion. "Come away in and sit you down," she invited courteously. "I am just about to lay the table."

"Let me help," offered Chrisann, and, as Jean opened her mouth to refuse, added, "please, Jean, it's the least I can do to thank you for your kind invitation."

"But, Miss," protested Jean, "Ullin is after telling us you are a fancy model and a cover girl. Setting tables is not for the likes of you."

Chrisann gave a delighted laugh. "Jean, in London I live all by myself in a flat. I am *used* to washing dishes and cooking meals for myself. Really, Jean, there's nothing special about me at all."

Jean gave a heartfelt sigh of relief and soon she and Chrisann were pottering companionably about the kitchen. It was a lovely big room with a well-polished range, the mantelshelf of which was covered with photographs. One of them was of a smiling young girl who looked like Mary and with a tug at her heart Chrisann guessed it was Jamie's mother.

Just after midday everyone came piling in; Claire to drape herself elegantly in a chintz-covered armchair, Kirsty to wash her hands before going to help Jean. The men all but stood in a queue by the sink to wash. Ullin had come in with Jamie on his shoulders. It was obvious the little boy adored the man, he copied everything he did, even to the extent of stripping to the waist to soap himself energetically.

Chrisann's heart flipped over at sight of Ullin's broad shouldered upper body. His chest was deeply bronzed and furred with fine golden hair, his brown arms rippled with muscles. Despite herself she couldn't stop herself from thinking about the intimacies that they had shared, the fierce possessive strength of his arms, the firm warm touch of his lips on hers. She gave herself a shake and whispered to Kirsty, "Isn't Mary here?"

"She works in a shop at Tobermory and has her lunch there. She'll be doing some shopping today, no doubt, last minute things before her wedding on Saturday. Will you be here for it? There's nothing to beat an island wedding."

Chrisann sighed and said wistfully, "I'd love to come but I'm afraid I must get back to London quite soon or my agent will have a fit, also I promised I would spend some time with my parents in Oban."

Kirsty looked at her ruefully. "What a pity, I was just beginning to enjoy having you around. You will be here for the Mull Highland Games though, they're on Thursday. That's why we're rushing around to get as many of the sheep done as we can because everyone goes to the games."

"That sounds marvellous," enthused Chrisann and

added hesitantly, "couldn't I help with the sheep this afternoon, I could do some of the unskilled stuff?"

Kirsty grinned and held out her hand. "Done," she said warmly and Chrisann giggled as they shook hands.

Mary's brother, Bob, a good-looking burly young man with a mop of dark hair, had already given Chrisann a shy but admiring appraisal. Now he pulled out a chair for her and she flashed him a smile as she sat down. Colin Mor said grace in his lilting voice and Chrisann felt strangely moved by the simplicity of the ritual, though she was annoyed to see that Claire had no such sentiments, making it quite plain that she thought the whole thing a joke by smothering a laugh as the family bowed their heads.

She could be very charming though and during the meal she proved too that she had a droll sense of humour as she described to Jean one or two funny incidents that had taken place that morning. But her remarks were directed at everyone except Chrisann whom she pointedly ignored. Chrisann was very conscious of Ullin's eyes on her and rather than face the mocking amusement in them she kept her eyes glued firmly on the plateful of steak and kidney that Jean had served up. Why, oh why did the man make her so acutely aware of his virile presence? She felt hot and uncomfortable and was glad when the talk veered round to the forthcoming Mull Games. It seemed that Ullin was to be a judge at one of the heavy events.

Claire's voice cut in, remarking that while she enjoyed the Games she much preferred the Military Tattoo in Edinburgh. "I so enjoyed it last year," she said dreamily. "Do you remember, Ullin, walking along Princes Street at sunset with the castle etched against the sky? Shall we stay at the North British again this year? The atmosphere is so elegant and the food divine."

"You've got expensive tastes, Claire," observed Bob rather wonderingly.

"The best for the best," she dimpled with a toss of her chestnut mane. "And Ullin knows how to treat a woman, don't you darling?"

Although Jean's cooking was perfection Chrisann found it sticking in her throat, but she couldn't hurt Jean and forced herself to eat. She was determined that come what may she wouldn't give Claire the satisfaction of knowing that her remarks, implying an intimate relationship with Ullin, had struck home and she certainly wouldn't let the beastly blond brute guess it either.

She was sorry for the tragedies that had been in his life, she was furious with herself for having made those remarks about his wife but she also felt that they couldn't have been so far off the mark. He was too selfish, arrogant and conceited to be ever able to love a woman warmly and unselfishly. Kirsty had said he adored her mother but a man like Ullin could easily mistake pure physical desire for love – and he was supremely physical. His animal-like sexual needs oozed out of every pore in his magnificent body. If that was the kind of love that Claire wanted she was asking for everything that was coming to her.

After the meal was over Chrisann thankfully scraped back her chair and rushed into the kitchenette to run the water for the dishes. Jean came in at her back and immediately protested but Chrisann would have none of it.

"You're a good lass," said Jean seriously. "I like a body who can make do with the highs and the lows."

"The highs and the lows?"

Jean blushed. "Ach, you know what I mean, the highbrows and the working classes. To tell the truth I was a wee bit worried about you coming here for lunch but it was a pleasure to have you."

"Oh, Jean, you're a gem," laughed Chrisann. "As for the working classes, I'm one of them. Oh, my job might sound very glamorous and it very often is but it also entails a lot of hard work and it's been wonderful to get away from it all for a while."

"That's what I like to hear," nodded Jean. "You won't be going back to the city before Saturday, I hope. Mary was saying she would like it if you came to the wedding. With you being a model you could help her make herself look really nice. In fact, why don't you come and stay with us for a few days, there's a spare bed in Mary's room if you don't mind sharing – it was Morag's bed. She was my eldest daughter but . . ."

Chrisann put her hand on Jean's arm and said quietly, "I know about it, Jean, Kirsty told me."

Jean fumbled with the ties of her apron. "Ay, she was a good girl though some may talk – Mary misses her and would dearly love it if you spent a few nights here. She came home last night bursting to tell us all about you. It would be fine for me too. There's so much to be done before Saturday and I'll miss a whole day on Thursday."

"Jean, you've just got yourself another wedding guest," said Chrisann rashly. "If I can use your phone I'll get through to London this very minute and let my agent know not to expect me back for a while."

Chrisann was almost deafened by Anthony's yells of rage when she told him of her intentions. She waited till the tirade was over then she said sweetly, "Anthony, a few more days won't hurt, I'm due a holiday and there's so much I want to see here the few measly days I've already had aren't nearly enough for all I want to do. . . ."

Carefully she laid the phone down on his further cries

of outrage then she went to seek out Jean to say, "That's that, I'm staying."

"Well, just you bring your things over whenever you want. Oh, Mary will be pleased, and I'm sure you'll enjoy yourself on Saturday – especially at the reception afterwards. It's to be at Strathullin House and a fine do it will be – Ullin will see to that."

Chrisann's senses reeled. She had already been made a fool of by Ullin MacBeth. He had walked out of his own house to sleep in a shepherd's cottage because he didn't want his so-called good reputation tarnished and she had vowed to herself that she would never again allow herself to be obliged to him. Yet she couldn't back out of her promises to Jean; the only course open to her now was to keep as much distance between them as was possible in the circumstances.

Saying her goodbyes to Jean she ran to join the others on their way to the fanks. Claire saw her and raised her eyebrows but she said nothing, for which Chrisann was thankful as she felt she couldn't take more snide remarks without showing how much they could strike home. The sheep surged inside the pens and very soon the air was reeking of antiseptic but to Chrisann it wasn't an unpleasant smell and she didn't mind in the least when Kirsty assigned her some of the more mundane tasks connected with dipping.

It was a very hot afternoon with the sun glinting on the blue water beyond the fields. The men were stripped to the waist and Chrisann looked covertly at Ullin, so magnificently male with the sun glinting on his fair hair and the perspiration gleaming on his broad bare back. He looked up and his eyes caught hers and she couldn't help flushing as she perceived his slow, impudent appraisal of her amateurish attempts at working with sheep. Claire on the other hand was as efficient as any of the men and she too flicked Chrisann a look of amused tolerance and said something to Ullin in a low voice.

Jean had packed sandwiches and tea for everyone and during the break Chrisann sat with Kirsty, their backs against a heathery knoll. Chrisann gazed at the panorama of sea and sky and gave a small but audible sigh.

"Are you tired?" asked Kirsty.

"No, I've enjoyed today – in fact – it's been wonderful, I feel for the first time in my life that I'm close to the earth and I hate the thought of having to go back to the city."

"Must you?" Kirsty sounded serious. "Is there someone standing over you telling you that the things you've been conditioned to do are the things you must keep doing all your life? If you turned your back on modelling would it be such a disaster?"

"If only it was that simple, Kirsty. My life is in London, my friends are there. I can't just turn my back on it all as if it never existed. Besides – what would I do here? I'm hardly an expert on the land."

"You could learn," Kirsty persisted. "And you could grow to love it."

In an effort to change the subject Chrisann said with a laugh, "Oh well, at least I've managed to wangle another few days here. Jean persuaded me to go to Mary's wedding. I left my agent having a blue fit on the phone. I'm going to help Mary look really super for her wedding day so I'm moving my things into her room. . . ."

Immediately she realized she'd made another blunder. Kirsty had asked her to stay at Dykehill and she had refused and she simply couldn't explain to Kirsty her reasons for doing so.

"I see." Kirsty turned away, her fair skin flushed with annoyance and Chrisann bit her lip as she realized that like it or not, she was becoming more and more enmeshed in the lives of people she hadn't known existed a week ago.

"I'm sorry, Kirsty," she apologized desperately. "Please believe me when I say that it has nothing at all to do with you – it – oh hell! I just feel so much for Jean and everything she's suffered and she does look as if she could be doing with some help. I may not be very good with sheep but as fashion is my profession I could really be of some help to Jean and Mary."

Kirsty immediately turned a repentant face. "You're right, of course, I am a selfish beast. I'll stay on Ronnach for a few more days and come over to Jean's in the evenings. I like Mary and we could all have a good giggle experimenting with make-up and hair styles."

Chrisann laughed with relief. "Great – and from the way I smell right now I think I'll have to experiment with soap and water to make me feel human again."

Kirsty hugged her knees and laughed too. "There's nothing wrong with the smell of grass and sheep dip. You could patent it and call it 'holiday discovery'. It might set off a whole new trend in the scent industry."

They both shrieked with laughter and went off in the best of spirits to resume work.

That evening, after a late dinner at the Scott's house, Chrisann walked over the sweet smelling machair to her little camp site. Her clothes were bone dry and she quickly packed them into a carrier bag before emerging from the tent to stand and absorb the wonder of her surroundings. The sea was a sheet of flame merging to gold near the shore where a statuesque heron stood in the shallows. The sky was a vast plain of rose, the horizon was brushed with silver.

Some distance away she saw the figure of a man standing at the water's edge, a statue of bronze etched against the sky, his hair a pale gold in the afterglow. Her heart thundered against her ribcage. It was Ullin, waiting for her – like – like a predator of the jungle, a magnificent tiger waiting to pounce on its prey – no – no – not that, her heart cried out! This was no jungle creature who hunted only to survive – this was a man, dynamic, powerful, possessed with such a potent aura of sexual desire he hunted only to conquer and, much as she loathed him for his vain, self-confident air of superiority, much as she utterly despised him for making her feel humiliated and degraded at every turn, she couldn't deny to herself any longer that she was helpless when she was in the fierce possessive circle of his arms.

Even to look at him made her heart beat strangely and feel acutely conscious of the erotic needs he had aroused in her body. She had never felt such overwhelming desire for a man before and it horrified her to know that she could want a man whose only obvious intention was to take her without the act being made beautiful by feelings of love and warmth.

She couldn't trust herself to let him touch her again; she mustn't allow herself to be alone with him again because she knew she wasn't strong enough to resist him. She turned and stumbled along the shore towards the road, her heart hammering in case he should turn and see her creeping away like a timid puppy. The cool night air against her face did nothing to lessen the fire in her cheeks and when she arrived back at the Scott's house it was to be greeted by Kirsty observing laughingly, "Chrisann, you're burning. You must have had too much of the sun."

"Have you been here long?" Chrisann heard herself asking faintly.

"Just five minutes. Dad went off with Mirk for a walk on the shore. Didn't you see him?"

"I was busy packing my things," answered Chrisann evasively, thankful that Mary arrived on the scene just then. Soon all three girls were having a blissful time experimenting with make-up watched by an interested Jamie who, after an initial spell of shyness, was soon chatting away to Chrisann, telling her how much he was looking forward to starting school which was situated at the Ronnach Ferry road junction and meant a journey twice daily by boat.

Mary's husband-to-be, a lanky young crofter with a friendly grin, arrived just as a face pack was being applied to Mary's face and in the laughter and banter that followed Chrisann cast all thoughts of Ullin from her mind. But later, when Mary was asleep, Chrisann slipped from her bed and went to stand by the window. The moon had risen in a cloudless sky, and she glimpsed in the distance the silvered sea. The secret shadows of night lay over the peaceful fields and she held her breath in wonder. A tiny glimmer of light caught her eye against the slopes of the hills and she knew it came from a window of Dykehill, that sturdy grey weatherbeaten house standing in the lee of a heather-covered knoll.

A great sense of yearning clawed inside her breast and despite the cool air seeping in through the open window a spear of warmth flooded through her. Soon she must leave Ronnach, soon she would leave behind the divine, dreamlike peace of the hills and the sea, but most of all she would soon leave behind the disturbing, unsettling presence of Ullin MacBeth and all the feelings of anger and mistrust he created in her. Yet even as she told herself this she knew she would never be free of him. Wherever she went, whatever she did, life for her would never be the same again and she hated him for the unrest she felt and the aching physical desires she experienced every time she remembered the intimate pressure of his lips on hers and the demanding hardness of his superb body coaxing hers to the warm sweet brink of total submission.

Chapter Seven

Chrisann felt a thrill running through her as she stood on Tobermory pier listening to the pipe band, celebrating the Mull Games, and watching the steamers spilling hundreds of visitors on Mull soil. She had come in Kirsty's little green mini and had been enchanted with everything she saw on the journey. Ullin had left early that morning and the Scotts had followed behind Kirsty in their ancient Volvo Estate.

The pipe band struck up once more and began to move along the main street, led by Lord Maclean of Duart Castle, chief of the clan Maclean. Behind him strode a giant of a man with hair the colour of ripe wheat, dressed in a lovat green tweed jacket and the MacBeth kilt. Chrisann's heart lurched at the splendid sight of Ullin MacBeth in his Highland regalia. No man had the right to look so devastatingly handsome, she thought, while she fought to put on a nonchalant smile as Kirsty grabbed her hand and made her run to join the crowds marching behind the band.

It was another glorious morning with the sun glinting on Tobermory Bay and the day that followed was as spectacular as the weather, full of excitement, colour and uninhibited merriment. The field was a natural amphitheatre high on a hill behind Tobermory and afforded a superb view of the deep blue Sound of Mull and the massed heat-hazed ranks of mainland hills.

Chrisann and Kirsty couldn't help smiling at the excited antics of Colin Mor and Bob who were so carried away by some of the heavy events they were unconsciously imitating the actions of the competitors. Yet even while she laughed Chrisann's eyes were seeking out Ullin, only just glimpsing him occasionally, through the crowd. Then she stiffened as she caught sight of Claire, tall, poised, superbly cool-looking in a mint green dress that hugged her waist but swirled seductively round her shapely legs.

She came towards them and acknowledged them graciously though she didn't look at Chrisann, who was feeling acutely aware of the fact that her limited choice of clothes didn't exactly stamp her as being a well-known fashion model. She had brought swimwear, T-shirts, shorts and jeans, thinking that was all she would need for a camping trip. At the last moment she had hastily thrown in an evening dress thinking she might need it if she had the good luck to participate in an island ceilidh, never dreaming that she would be wearing it to an island wedding reception. There was still the question of what to wear to the actual wedding and she half thought of going to see if there was anything suitable in the Tobermory shops but Kirsty told her it was a holiday for almost everyone for miles around.

"Well, I'll have to go to Oban tomorrow," said Chrisann desperately. "I feel an absolute mess."

"You can't go tomorrow," said Kirsty placidly. "It's Jean's birthday and Dad has planned to take us all out to Staffa in *Happy Days*."

"Happy Days?"

"His boat; we're planning on a picnic. I've made a birthday cake for Jean. . . ."

They had reached the tea tent by now and Chrisann

stopped short to say, "Who exactly is inviting me to this picnic . . . ?"

"I am." Ullin's cool, self-assured voice at her elbow made her jump and whirl round to almost collide with him. His hand shot out to grip her elbow and she felt his flesh burning into her and his blue eyes piercing into hers as if he could read every thought that passed through her head. He had shed his jacket and his crisp, dazzling white shirt, was a startling contrast against his mahogany skin.

Something seemed to clutch at her very breath so that she stammered, "Are you indeed? Well, I shan't be coming, I have to do some shopping."

His eyes mocked her as he drawled, "What, and disappoint Jean? I told her this morning you were coming. You can't go gallivanting off to town at such a busy time. Jean wasn't going to accept the chance of a birthday treat but I reminded her she had you to help out and when she thought it over she was delighted."

Kirsty had slipped into the tent to fetch the tea and with crimson cheeks Chrisann hissed at Ullin, "You think you have us all under your control, don't you? You really believe you can manipulate everyone into obeying your arrogant assumptions."

"I can," he returned calmly, "especially you, Chrisann."

From the dim interior of the tea tent Chrisann saw Claire's amber eyes watching her with ill-concealed dislike and she decided that under no circumstances would she make a fool of herself by losing her temper. Far better to keep as calm as she could and in so doing play both Ullin and Claire at their own game. Going into the tent she declared audibly, "Thank you, Mr MacBeth, I shall be delighted to accept your invitation for tomorrow afternoon. I must, however, get Mary a wedding gift, also something for myself to wear at her wedding so I'll get an early boat over to Oban and be back in time for the picnic."

Claire's eyes flicked casually over the lemon T-shirt and shorts worn by Chrisann and with a charming smile she commented, "It would certainly never do to attend a wedding dressed like that and you a fashion model." Turning her back deliberately she curled her long fingers possessively round Ullin's arm and drawing him down beside her smiled into his eyes. "Darling, take your tea before it gets cold." She glanced at her watch and sighed. "I really must be getting along. I promised Aunt Rose I would go and have tea at her house and with her being an invalid she gets cantankerous and I don't want to do anything to upset her." She lifted her lips ruefully. "The old dear would cut me out of her will if I didn't pay these duty calls now and again."

Returning with a tray of tea and a plateful of buttered pancakes Kirsty said sweetly, "You would suffer anything for the sake of money, Claire. Your Aunt Rose is a dear old lady and your visits to her shouldn't be regarded simply as duty calls."

Claire merely smiled. "Such wisdom on young shoulders – but you're right of course. Aunt Rose is a dear – she's also loaded and has no one but me and her cats to leave her money to." She snuggled closer to Ullin. "Now that you're more or less clear of the work load on Ronnach you won't be staying at Dykehill for the time being, will you, darling? I'll expect you at Stonehurst for dinner tonight and no excuses."

"We'll be starting on the dipping over on this side," he pointed out with an indulgent laugh.

"Oh, you work far too hard for someone of your standing – what on earth do you keep tenants for if not to look after things for you?"

"I enjoy doing what I do. I was a farmer before I was a landlord, it's in my blood."

She pouted. "Well, you needn't think you have to work tonight. I'll expect you around eight. We can have a lovely cosy meal together and I'm sure we'll find plenty to do to occupy ourselves afterwards."

She stood up and bending low to expose the full cleavage of her breasts she kissed him full on the lips then with a toss of her chestnut mane she made an elegant exit from the tea tent.

Kirsty gave an audible sigh of relief and said eagerly, "I've just met an old school chum and she wants me to meet her after the Games and have a meal somewhere." She turned to Chrisann. "Only thing is it means I won't be able to take you back to Ronnach Ferry, but you're welcome to join us. I told Joan about you and she would love to meet a famous fashion model."

Chrisann hesitated. She was hot and tired and didn't particularly relish an evening of discussion about her profession. She wanted to forget it for a while but, as the Scotts' car would be full to bursting, there was nothing else for it but to go with Kirsty.

But Ullin had other ideas. He pounced before she could open her mouth, his tones crisp. "Chrisann can come in my car. I'll finish up as quickly as I can here."

"Oh well, I suppose it's for the best," agreed Kirsty. "Joan tends to prattle a bit and might get you down, Chrisann."

"That's settled then," said Ullin, getting to his feet. "Wait at the car for me, Chrisann, I left it in the shade so if you feel too hot you can sit inside till I come."

He extracted a set of keys from the pocket of his jacket and threw them at her. As she caught them she wanted to scream, "That is *not* settled, Ullin MacBeth." But she could hardly do so in the crowded tea tent, or anywhere for that matter, for she had no intention of letting anyone guess how much she despised Ullin. She would keep her dignity at all costs even if Ullin seemed hell bent on trying to determine that she kept nothing else.

On the homeward journey she was thankful that he had little to say. Silently he guided the comfortable Rover over the narrow moorland road, one bronzed arm resting on the window ledge, the other just inches from her knee as he smoothly changed gears. Though she sat jammed against the door in order to be as far from contact with him as possible she was so conscious of his nearness she had to fight down an almost irresistible urge to lay her hand over his long mobile fingers, to stroke the golden hairs glinting on the back of his hand. He had slung his jacket onto the back seat and had loosened the tartan tie at his throat so that the collar of his white shirt lay open, exposing the firm brown flesh of his chest.

In the shimmering distance she spotted the grey towers of a house nestling in the luxuriant depths of acres of fertile land. She hadn't noticed it on the outgoing journey that morning and she cried out in delight, "What a beautiful place – and the house, it's so – so noble."

"It is," he agreed quietly. "Very noble and fine – wonderful grazing land too. It's Stonehurst – Claire's place."

"I see," she murmured, "And you mean to get your hands on it?"

"If it's at all possible," he said amiably.

"A package deal," she couldn't stop herself saying bitterly. "Claire wants what you've got and you want Stonehurst."

He turned a cold quizzical stare on her. "I likened you once to a vixen, Chrisann; I was wrong, you're a cat."

Rage engulfed her, rage at herself for her unthinking words and she huddled into her corner, hating him for his superior attitude and his knack of always having the last word at her expense. They drove for a few more miles in silence and even though she longed to ask him to show her where the Strathullin Estate lay she wouldn't give him the satisfaction of thinking that she was even remotely interested.

"Why are you afraid of me?" he asked, suddenly and tersely.

"Afraid of you?" she quavered. "Don't flatter yourself."

"I don't have to, I find that women manage it very successfully," he said with such assurance she could have hit him very gladly. "You flatter me, Chrisann, you're so afraid to come near me you crept away the other night because you couldn't trust yourself to be alone with me."

"How can you possibly bear to be so conceited?" she gasped with a glance at his handsome profile.

A smile lifted his mouth as he said, "Not conceited, Chrisann, truthful, and I'm going to prove it to you before very long."

She glanced around nervously at the vast stretches of empty moor on either side and said faintly, "You wouldn't dare—"

"Oh, but I would," he cut in brusquely. "And no matter how much you think you might fight me you would surrender in the end. However, you will have to wait a while longer for such a test of physical endurance. . . ." He flicked up his wrist and glanced at his watch. "I must get out of these things and have a bath. . . ."

"Oh, yes, you simply must look your best for Claire," she spat and could have bitten out her tongue.

But he carried on smoothly, as if she hadn't spoken. "In time for dinner – also . . ." he turned his head and the blue eyes regarded her with mocking amusement, "I must get everything ready for tomorrow; if the weather holds it should be quite a day."

At Ronnach Ferry he arranged for her to be taken over to the island and as he climbed back into the car he said laconically, "Don't forget to bring your swimsuit tomorrow." His eyes ran over her slender figure. "I think I'm entitled to see more of you as a reward for coming out of my way to bring you here." With that he turned the car and disappeared over the winding road leaving Chrisann seething with hatred and frustration.

Next morning she borrowed the Scotts' Volvo and spent a rushed two hours in Oban, guilt seizing her because she hadn't the time to even pop in and say hallo to her mother. To compensate slightly she dived into her father's shop to let him know she would see him and her mother the following week then she made a mad dash to the midday ferry which she caught by the skin of her teeth.

She arrived back at Ronnach Ferry to find everyone gathered at the slipway ready to be off. She slipped Jean the gift of a silver Celtic cross she had purchased in her father's shop and hugging her wished her a happy birthday. Jean was overwhelmed and turned quickly to climb into the big rowing boat beside Kirsty, Jamie and Claire. Colin Mor and Bob had opted out of the trip as the Mull Games had put them behind with their work. Mary too had many last minute details to see to and was shopping in Tobermory. Even so, the party of six filled the rowing boat manned by Ullin with a willing Jamie ready to attend to any small tasks that came to hand.

Claire looked magnificent with her shining hair swept up showing to advantage her slender neck and the delicate curve of her shoulders. She was sitting at the stern, lazily trailing her fingers in the silken green water, the secretive smile that curved her lips reminding Chrisann of a pampered cat who had just feasted on cream. Chrisann pulled her gaze away from the self-satisfied-looking mistress of Stonehurst and tried not to imagine what sort of evening Ullin had spent whilst in her company.

They neared the white launch Chrisann had first noticed on her arrival at Ronnach Ferry. The name *Happy Days* was emblazoned in black edged with gold, enhancing further the sleek, expensive-looking vessel. Very soon they were all aboard and away, the bow cutting a frothing trough through the waves. The sun was high and very warm and the sky was blue and unclouded. The sea was so calm it reflected the terraced hills of Ronnach and those of the Mull coast.

Chrisann gazed back to see Ben More, its head completely clear of cloud. Ullin pointed out the isles of Gometra, Iona, Staffa, and Little Colonsay, then the ethereal shapes of the Treshnish group: Fladda as green as an emerald; the terraced mound of Lunga; the two Cairnna Burgh Begs; the conical outline of the Dutchman's Cap and the amazing Harp Rock with its colonies of sea-birds. On the rocks offshore, dozens of seals basked in the sun while clouds of Terns rose into the sky.

Ullin guided the boat to Lunga and anchored offshore. "This is a good spot if anyone cares to swim," he commented carelessly. His eyes sought Chrisann's in an unspoken challenge and she was thankful that she was a reasonably competent swimmer.

She had put on her swimsuit beneath her outer garments before leaving Ronnach that morning and now she stripped off her T-shirt and jeans. Kirsty and Claire did likewise, the former dancing over to Chrisann to say admiringly, "No wonder you're a model, what a figure." She pinched herself round the middle and said ruefully, "I'll have to get rid of my puppy fat, though not today; I'm looking forward to the feast in that hamper."

She was a picture with her fair hair tossing in the breeze and the flush of sunburn on her skin and Chrisann brought out a bottle of suntan lotion and said severely, "You put some of that on after your swim or you'll end up with blisters."

Claire, dazzling in a pink bikini, was standing poised, ready to dive, though she waited till Ullin emerged from below before she made a perfect cut into the water. Kirsty followed her but Chrisann found her way blocked by Ullin's outflung arm. Her breath caught in her throat for he was taller and more superbly male than ever in a pair of blue swim briefs that were stretched tightly over his loins. His muscular legs were long and lithe and she found herself staring at the fair hairs on his thighs because she simply couldn't bring herself to look into his eyes.

"Well, well, well," he drawled admiringly, "what a pity you didn't get a chance to wear that sooner." She threw her head up then only to feel burning blushes of embarrassment spreading over her face and neck as his eyes travelled over the length of her legs, lingered for what seemed like aeons on her shapely waist, before coming to rest on the fullness of her creamy breasts rising above the low-cut top of her cerise satin costume.

"Stop that," she hissed, nervously looking towards Jean who seemed to have fallen asleep in her deck chair.

"Stop what?" His blue orbs held her furious glare. "Surely it's no sin to admire a beautiful girl when the opportunity arises."

"Well – admire her then," she stammered, with a toss of her head indicating Claire expertly cleaving the waves.

"Ah, it's like that," he nodded with an infuriatingly calm smile. "I'm being told in a roundabout way that what you thought was mine last night mustn't be allowed to get cold."

"Oh – go to hell!" she choked and flounced away from him to make such a clumsy dive into the water she almost landed on top of Claire who voiced her disapproval in no uncertain terms.

On the journey to Staffa, Claire snuggled against Ullin as he stood in the wheelhouse and Chrisann was silent as she towelled her hair and watched the amazing formation of rock looming closer. It was an awesome sight and she stared at the volcanic island with its basaltic pillars and great yawning caverns. Ullin dropped anchor and they all climbed into the rowing boat. "We're lucky," he observed, pulling strongly at the oars. "We've come in a quiet spell and as it's half-tide we'll be able to get into Fingal's Cave."

They landed and made their way over a causeway of pillars towards the great arch of the famous cave. Claire held tightly to Ullin's hand and Jamie clung to the other one as they made their way inside.

"It goes so far back," Chrisann observed in awe to Kirsty, who supplied the information that the cave was two hundred and twenty-seven feet in length and sixty feet high at that particular tide. Chrisann felt as if she was entering an ancient Greek temple. Lights danced and flickered over golden lichens growing on the pillars. The sea was crystal clear and was turquoise and pink near the rocks with glimpses of vivid blue where the medusae clustered. The subterranean boom of the Atlantic echoed through the vast cavern together with the cries of hundreds of seabirds. It was overwhelming, beautiful, frightening and utterly awe-inspiring. Chrisann believed she was living through one of the most wonderful experiences of her life. The melody of untamed forces was all around her, and she felt that no matter what happened to her in the future, she would remember this day for the rest of her life.

The others were making their way back to the entrance but in a daze of enchantment Chrisann plunged on. All about her there was tumult; the thunderous might of wave upon rock; the swelling screams of the gulls. She went to the edge of the walkway and peered down into the foaming green depths below which mesmerized her even as her stomach lurched.

"Chrisann!" Ullin's voice reverberated.

She gasped and gazed desperately over her shoulder to see him coming towards her. With a start she realized the others had gone outside and she was alone in Fingal's Cave with Ullin MacBeth. She stumbled and her foot slipped on the wet rock. His hand shot out to jerk her back from the edge and he said harshly, "Little fool, don't you know that water has currents that could suck you down and smash you on the rocks!"

"Don't you dare call me a fool, Ullin MacBeth!" she cried on a half-sob. "Never lay a finger on me again. . . ."

He yanked her towards him and she slithered and would have fallen but for his powerful arms hauling her upright.

"How dare you?" she panted. "You – you barbarian." Like lightning her hand flashed out and cracked him across the cheek but she might as well have struck a piece of rock so slight was the impression she made. For a moment he remained motionless but his jaw was tight and his eyes were snapping like firecrackers.

She was afraid of the ire she had induced in him and defensively she gasped, "Don't touch me, I warn you, you have no right. Who are you anyway? Just a man like all the—"

His grip tightened on her wrists. "I think I might be

the man who's about to tame you!" he gritted through clenched teeth.

She fought him like a tigress, her long nails raking through the furring of hair on his chest to the skin beneath. "Please, please, don't," she whimpered.

"Oh yes, Chrisann, you can't fight me any more – you don't want to." Roughly he pulled her towards him and crushed her body to his. His hands on her naked shoulders were like brand burns, his lips on hers hard and seeking. She sobbed and struggled but he held tight. The warm moistness of his tongue probed into her mouth. She went limp in his arms as a spear of fire seared through her. Now she didn't want to fight him, she wanted only to be in his arms, to feel the ecstasy of his lips on hers.

The kisses went deeper and deeper, sweet, and passionate. And she was responding, arching her back so that her body was moulded ever more intimately to his. She wound her arms round his back and shivered with delight at the feel of his firm flesh. Now he was stroking her body, his fingers leaving a tingling trail of fire down her spine before seeking the soft flesh curving over the top of her swimsuit . . . and then he was cupping the firm swelling roundness of her breasts, caressing the hardness of her nipples through the fine satin material of her swimsuit, his fingers sliding expertly, manipulatively till she gave a little moan of delight and closed her eyes as an unbelievable tremor of sensual longing surged inside her.

His kisses went ever deeper and she clung to him with unashamed passion as he went wild, his muscular thighs enclosing her soft buttocks while he pushed the thin straps of her costume down over her shoulders. She had no resistance left now, all her resolutions crumbled away and she was so lost in a drowning wave of erotic excitement she felt as if he and she were one and while her senses whirled she wanted only to be always in his hard demanding arms and to feel the delicious brutal power of his masculine body crushing hers. . . .

Quite suddenly he released her and running his fingers through his hair he said softly, "We can't play games like this here—"

"Games!" she cut in. "Oh yes, that's all a relationship between a man and woman would mean to you." Feeling weak with reaction she leaned back against the rough surface of the cave and raced on, "You're despicable," she panted, "and a boorish brute into the bargain! I suppose it amuses you to use that monstrous strength of yours against a defenceless woman—"

"Defenceless! That's a good one! That was a pretty hefty right swing you landed on my face." He lowered his head and looked at the scratches on his chest. "And these, hardly the work of a weakling."

"Did you think I was just going to stand there and let you maul me? What do you take me for? These aren't the Dark Ages you know. Women nowadays are no longer submissive idiots who believe themselves to have been created for man's pleasure alone—"

"You could have fooled me," he cut in brusquely. "You loved every minute of being in my arms just now and if I hadn't stopped in time I really do believe you would have let me do anything with you – right here – with people about to come in at any moment."

"I don't hear anyone," she said dazedly, but he was right, voices came from the entrance; a boatload of tourists had arrived.

He grabbed her hand roughly and said, "Come on, let's get out of here, the others will be waiting."

"You go on," she told him, only wanting time to compose herself before meeting Claire's questioning eyes but his hand tightened on hers till she winced and cried out. "Let me go – or – I'll – I'll scream."

"You will not, I'm not having you throwing tantrums in front of people."

"Oh yes, I forgot, that precious reputation of yours!" she shouted, then jumped in fright as her voice reverberated through the cave with terrifying effect.

"You have just had a tantrum!" he gritted and drew her back down the walkway like a naughty child. She squirmed and dug in her heels but it was useless. In the end she had to give in and was forced to run in order to keep up with him. Once outside he abruptly let her go and miserably she followed him to the grassy plateau above the rocks where Jean and Kirsty had laid out the picnic. Claire threw her a look of utter dislike and observed haughtily, "You *do* keep Ullin busy rescuing you, Chrisann. You were both so long I was beginning to think you must have drowned down there."

Chrisann was about to hurl back a derogatory reply but bit the words back. This was Jean's day and she wasn't going to let Claire or Ullin spoil it. With a forced attempt at jollity she went to sit on the grass beside Jamie who was in a welter of impatience to have the cake cut and the picnic begun.

Chrisann had no appetite but forced herself to eat. Under no circumstances would she let that hateful man see how much he had upset her. She dreaded tomorrow evening when she would have to give every appearance of enjoying herself under the roof of Strathullin House, but she would be careful not to be alone for one minute with the arrogant beast who so obviously thought himself to be lord and master of all he surveyed.

Chapter Eight

Most of the guests had arrived at Strathullin House having come straight from the church just a few miles away. The womenfolk of Ronnach had brought any necessities with them in order to avoid going back to the island and Chrisann stood before the mirror in Kirsty's room, thankful that her dress was none the worse for the soaking it had received during the storm. She had ironed out all the creases and the folds of flame-coloured silk clung to her slender curves and showed her dark hair to startling advantage. Nervously she smoothed down the skirt and wished she had brought something that didn't reveal her shoulders, but in the next instant she decided it didn't matter. Claire would no doubt arrive looking like a dream and Ullin would have plenty to keep his eyes occupied.

A glowing Mary danced in dressed in a pink suit that matched the pretty flush on her cheeks. "You look lovely, Chrisann," she enthused.

"So do you, Mary, and the wedding was the nicest I've ever attended."

"Your own will be the best," dimpled Mary.

"I doubt it," said Chrisann faintly. "I don't think I'll get married."

"You're kidding," said Mary disbelievingly. "The wonder is a lovely person like you has escaped it so long."

"Not everyone thinks of me in that way, Mary."

"No?" Mary slid her a sidelong glance. "I don't believe that for a minute. You must have loads of boyfriends waiting impatiently for your return to London."

Kirsty came in, looking sweet and very young in a pale blue dress. "Who wants to think about London tonight?" she grinned. "We're on Mull and an island wedding reception always turns out to be a ball. It's also a great excuse for everyone to catch up on all the gossip with relatives and friends. Jean and Colin Mor are surrounded by folk all pleading with them to spend the night and a few of them not taking no for an answer."

They moved out into the corridor and Chrisann shivered a little. She had been disappointed with her first sight of Strathullin House. It was a rambling ugly old mansion set in grounds which were mainly woodland. The interior of the house was somewhat gloomy and though it was a warm night the rooms were cold. But the crowded sitting-room was already hot. Guests stood in little knots everywhere, chatting animatedly, drinks in hand. People were drifting in and out of the dining-room where a cold buffet was spread invitingly.

Chrisann found herself searching the throng for Ullin. She despised herself for being so weak but she seemed to be caught up in a force that was without her control. She spotted him chatting easily to a large group. He was standing under the light which gleamed on the ripe wheat of his hair, his ruggedly handsome face was animated, and she heard his laugh ringing out. He was so tall and powerful he seemed to loom head and shoulders above every other man present but it was the forceful quality of the man which drew her eyes like a helpless scrap of metal to a magnet.

She turned her head away quickly and the vision of Claire floated in front of her, poised and perfectly coiffured, statuesque in a figure-hugging black dress with a very revealing neckline. She gazed at Chrisann through half-shut eyes and in a low voice said sweetly, "I see you've got your eye on the laird again, my dear. Really, you're so obvious. Men like women who have the breeding not to throw themselves." Caught off-guard like that Chrisann could think of nothing to say and Claire went on smoothly, "You don't fool anybody with all that maiden in distress stuff, you know. Personally I find it very embarrassing, after all, it surely must be plain to everyone that a girl like you, with all the experience of city life, isn't exactly the definition of a coy young thing. Believe me, Ullin has had too much experience with women to be taken in by you."

Chrisann's face was burning but before she could make any reply the other girl drifted unhurriedly away to entwine her arm through Ullin's and establish herself into his conversation.

Chrisann turned blindly away and was glad that Kirsty came up at that moment to take her on a tour of introduction. The names and faces were a blur in Chrisann's memory but she smiled and said all the right things. Drinks were being passed round and she took a glass and gulped the contents down before she was aware that it was whisky. Rashly she accepted another but sipped at it this time, aware that her face felt very hot.

Miserably she wandered out into the corridor and walked along in a haze, recalling Claire's cruel words. She felt a sob catching in her throat. The sooner she was off this island the better. She had to get back to the things she knew and understood. She was getting to the stage where she couldn't think straight, she had to get back to normality – before the influences of hatred and self-loathing bred in her by Ullin swamped her completely. With a mirthless laugh she swallowed the remaining contents in her glass and wandered aimlessly, the empty glass dangling in the crook of her fingers.

"I've been looking for you." Ullin's deep voice at her back completely unnerved her and the glass fell, rolling unbroken along the carpeted corridor. Stooping he picked it up and before she could make a move his bruising fingers were under her elbow, guiding her into a nearby room. The door clicked shut and she stared round her in panic. She was in a bedroom, large and airy, the curtains stirring in a breeze from the open window. Ullin spun her round to face him and there was anger in his voice when he said, "Where the hell did you think you were going? I tried to get over to you to do the introductions then I saw you with Kirsty – and after that you disappeared."

"Ullin, please, please leave me alone," she begged wearily. Her head was spinning and she knew she had taken the whisky too quickly. Her limbs felt leaden and she felt that she had no resistance left in her to fight him – she was tired – tired of it all – she had come to Mull for a rest and instead she seemed to have undergone one emotional battle after another. The room was cold after the heat of the sitting room and she began to tremble violently.

Instantly his arms were about her in a strong, protective embrace and when he spoke his voice was full of tender concern. "You're cold," he whispered into her hair. "Let me hold you in my arms and love you." His lips were warm against her neck and she wanted only to be held like that in his arms forever. She had never heard such gentleness in his voice and the undemanding hold of his arms about her waist wasn't characteristic of him. This entirely new approach was her undoing; she felt her throat constricting with unshed tears.

His words were falling like sweet cool rain in the stillness of the room. "Chrisann, you're so beautiful," he told her huskily. "When I saw you tonight you looked like a bright and fiery flame lighting the drabness of this house."

He pulled back to look deep into her eyes and she caught her breath on something that could only be described as an emotional pain. In the soft shadows of the room his eyes were dark pools, his hair a dusky gold, his rugged face soft and mysterious – but it was his lips that held her attention, firm, wide, so close. . . . She lifted a finger and traced their outline and as he gathered her once more into his arms she experienced a surge of pure wonder as he kissed her hair, her throat, and when he finally came to her mouth she was eager to meet his lips with hers. Tenderly he nuzzled her soft pliant mouth. Gone was all his usual savagery, instead the clasp that held her, though strong, was strangely relaxed and she found herself marvelling that such a virile man could be so gentle.

"Chrisann," he was murmuring her name, savouring the sound of it, then his mouth was on hers once more in a long lingering kiss.

She felt the world spinning away till it seemed it was just she and Ullin alone in the entire universe. In a mind shattering sensation of whirling through space to touch the stars it was as if time had stood still and these moments with Ullin would be locked in a divine eternity. His hands were caressing her soft curves while she delighted in touching his wonderfully firm muscular shoulders and back. Over and over they sighed each other's names and it seemed to Chrisann that the joyous enchantment would never stop. She was aware of Ullin's mounting desire but she didn't care because there was a burning ache inside herself, a craving for fulfilment such as she had never known before and she pressed herself ever closer to him till it seemed they were as one flesh, pulsating with heated desire.

"Beautiful, beautiful, Chrisann," he murmured huskily and in a dream she found herself being swept into his arms and she was being carried like a feather over the carpet to the bed and as he laid her down and moulded himself on top of her all the gentleness had left him and now he was an exciting hard creature filled with smouldering passion.

His demanding lips claimed hers over and over and she gave herself up to ecstasy, revelling in every fresh delight his strong expert fingers were invoking in her. His hands were whispering over the flimsy material of her dress, cupping her breasts, and she made no move to stop him as he slid the straps of her dress over her shoulders. A quiver ran through her as she felt her breasts being unfettered from their silken bonds. Her name was a hoarse whisper in these passion laden moments. He was lost, awash with desire and he was taking her with him to lands of unbelievable sensual pleasure. . . .

A stab of unease speared through her like a knife wound as Claire's voice came unbidden to her mind. "*Men like women not to throw themselves . . . you're so obvious, Chrisann. . . .*"

"No, Ullin," she protested feebly, though he had brought her body to such a pitch of craving she could hardly get the words out.

"Oh, but yes, Chrisann," he said harshly, his lips nuzzling her nipples. "You want me and I want you, you can't deny it any longer—"

"I can, I can," she sobbed in sudden fear. "This isn't love."

"This is what we have both wanted from the beginning, you're not going to tell me that isn't true."

She came blindingly and suddenly to her senses and

the fire went out of her to be replaced by anger. All he wanted was her body so that he could notch her up as another conquest; all along he had seen her as just another female to pursue and finally conquer. That was all she meant to him. He had boasted to her that she would surrender to him in the end and, fool that she was, she had almost capitulated to his arrogant assumptions.

Hatred for him swamped her once more and she tried to break free of his steel-like hold but with that mocking smile she knew so well he restrained her with contemptuous ease. Panic-stricken she fought him like a wild cat and quite suddenly he released her and stood up, his voice breaking across her ears like cracked ice as he said scornfully. "Why do you deny me – us – the thing that your body aches to have? Is it because you're afraid of yourself? That once awakened and fulfilled you will crave for more and more ecstasy – or are you so cold and prudish it goes against your grain to admit you have the same needs as every other human being. You're not a model, Chrisann – you're a tailor's dummy and I don't need a wax image in my life, thank you very much."

She recoiled from the seething fury in his voice and with a sob of utter self-loathing she got up and began to straighten her dress. "Go back to Claire," she threw at him wildly. "She's only too ready to give you everything you want – that much I've gathered even though, as you imply, I'm hardly human. Your reputation is at stake, Ullin MacBeth, though from your behaviour just now, one would hardly think so, nor from the way Claire bandies about all the cosy little sexual adventures you appear to have shared—"

"So that's it?" he rasped. "The claws are showing again, eh, Chrisann? At least Claire is a woman and doesn't mind admitting to it."

"She doesn't admit it – she boasts about it and if that's the sort of woman you want then you'll make a fine match for one another. Why don't you go to her now! I'm sure she'll be waiting with open arms."

"I might just bloody well do that!" he snarled and striding to the door he wrenched it open, throwing back savagely over his shoulder, "Don't be in too much of a hurry to show your face! My guests are enjoying themselves and I don't want you mooning around spoiling things for them."

The door banged and she crept to the mirror to comb her hair. Huge eyes and a white strained face looked back at her and hastily she tried to pinch some colour back into her cheeks, wishing she hadn't left her bag in Kirsty's room. Suddenly she decided to go and fetch it, and then get away from this house as quickly as she could; the quicker she left the despicable Ullin behind the better. She had to be rid of him for once and for all.

His mocking words rang in her ears as she went upstairs to retrieve her bag. She shuddered with hatred of him and her heart twisted with pain as the sting of his bitter words echoed and re-echoed in her head. She found Jean and said quickly, "Jean, if I take your car could you get a lift later? I – I feel a bit headachy."

"Of course, lass," said Jean kindly. "But you'll be all alone in the house because we have been asked to spend the night with some relatives. Kirsty was going to ask you to stay here."

"Tell her thanks but I'd really rather get back to Ronnach. I don't mind in the least staying in the house alone. I'll feed the hens in the morning so you don't have to hurry back."

"Ach, you're a good lass right enough," beamed Jean. "The keys are in the car and Dave will row you over to Ronnach."

Chrisann hurried away from the sounds of laughter. In the spacious entrance hall Claire was sitting on a wooden settle with a glass in her hand. Her amber eyes flicked over Chrisann and she drawled, "Leaving so soon?"

"Yes," answered Chrisann tightly.

Claire's manner changed and her voice was friendly as she said apologetically, "You mustn't mind the things I said back there – it's just . . ." She fingered her glass and said rather hesitantly, "To tell the truth I have been snappy lately. I went to see my doctor last week and – well – he confirmed something I have suspected for a while." Chrisann stared as the other girl went on. "It's true, so you do see, I have my reasons to worry a bit. . . ."

It was the last straw for Chrisann; she turned away from Claire and walked blindly to the Volvo parked in the driveway. The journey to Ronnach Ferry passed in a daze and she had little recollection of Dave rowing her over to the island. Her head was throbbing and she barely knew what she was doing.

For a long time she sat in the kitchen quite unable to take in the implications of Claire's words and it was past nine when she finally got up and made her way to the bathroom. There she ran a bath, undressed, and slid into the hot water to scrub furiously at herself, as if by doing so she could scrub away the memory of Ullin's touch.

Feeling as limp as a rag doll she donned jeans and a blouse and made her way back to the kitchen to put the kettle on. It was while she was waiting for it to boil she glanced through the window and saw Raymond Carstairs coming towards the house. He was picking his way over the shingle, intent on keeping his feet dry. He was dressed in a pale blue suit and an immaculate white shirt and in his hand was an overnight case.

Chrisann groaned. She couldn't take any more emotional

upsets that evening and throwing open the door she ran to intercept him. "Just what are you doing here, Raymond?" she asked tightly.

His dark eyes flicked over her appraisingly. "Now, now, darling, I know that tone and I don't want any tantrums. I've come to take you back, of course."

"Like hell you will! Who told you where I was?"

He brushed a speck of fluff from the lapel of his jacket. "Your mother. I phoned and asked if she knew where you were. At first she wasn't going to tell me but when I explained that I was your fiancé she changed her tune and directed me here."

Chrisann's nostrils flared. All the old familiar tensions spewed back into her muscles till she was rigid with indignation. "My fiancé! That's a despicable lie and you know it! How dare you interfere with my life? You had no right to come here."

"Oh, come on now, Chrisann," he murmured placatingly, "I've come quite a distance and I'm in no mood to be trifled with. I hired a car at Oban but had to leave it over at Ronnach Ferry. I managed to persuade an idle-looking fellow to bring me over, never dreaming he would bundle me into a filthy rowing boat. I stink of fish and I'm covered in oil—"

"Good!" cried Chrisann. "I'm glad you were put to some inconvenience but you're not through yet. You can just go back the way you came. You can stay in a hotel over on Mull and catch the first boat back in the morning."

But Raymond pretended not to hear. "I wonder, is there any place round here I might get a meal? I really am tired, Chrisann, and I did come a long way just to see you. You might show a bit of concern."

She looked at his dark heavy-jawed face. It was rather weary looking and she relented though her mind was racing desperately as she wondered where on earth he would sleep that night. Leading the way indoors she explained about the owners of the house, adding hesitantly that they wouldn't be arriving back till tomorrow. "Don't get any ideas though," she added hastily. "My camp bed is out in the shed. We'll bring it into the living-room for you."

As it turned out she was glad of Raymond's company. After a meal of bacon and eggs he stretched out thankfully in a comfortable armchair and gave her all the latest news surrounding the fashion scene and all the gossip about their particular circle of friends in the social world. The talk kept her mind off the things that had seethed in it since fleeing from Strathullin House. Later, when the camp bed was made up and Chrisann declared her intention of going to bed, Raymond looked at her seriously and said, "It really is wonderful to see you again, Chrisann, I've missed you . . . pity we have to go our separate ways when we have the house to ourselves. . . ."

"Look, I really am exhausted, and so must you be," she said quickly. "I hope you have a good night."

"Better if I had something to cuddle," he said gloomily. Before she could evade him he reached over and kissed her. His mouth was warm and soft and there was no demand behind the gesture. . . . Ullin burst into her thoughts and she remembered the hard, possessive pressure of his lips coaxing hers to respond. . . . She mustn't think about the loathsome creature – she mustn't. . . .

She stepped out of Raymond's reach. "Good-night," she said softly. "I have to be up early to see to things here but you can sleep on if you like." He was tired enough not to object to any of this and thankfully she escaped to make her way upstairs, missing Mary's cheerful presence in the room.

Though she was exhausted she slept fitfully and wakened at dawn to rise and go quietly down to the kitchen where she made tea. She sat at the table, lost in thought, wondering why she should feel such utter condemnation for the life-style of an expert womanizer whom she hated so deeply. . . . Her fingers tightened round her cup – hell how she hated him – but God! She needed him – no craved for him.

She had never felt such all-consuming passion for any man before – and that was all it was, a crude thirsting after sexual fulfilment with a man she despised. He had taken away all the illusions she had cherished in her heart about one day falling in love with a man who would love and protect her and bring her peace of mind. Ullin was the very opposite of such a dream, he was totally selfish, wanting only to satisfy his physical needs with any attractive woman that chanced along – as for peace of mind with him! She gave a mirthless little laugh. She had been tormented by him ever since that first meeting on Mull.

Even now, knowing the things that Claire had told her, she experienced a pang of hungry longing for the hard intimacy of his superb male body. . . . With an angry little cry of protest she got up and began cleaning out the fireplace; the kitchen was warm and breakfast ready when Raymond finally put in a belated appearance. He was quite enchanted with the island and they spent a pleasant day pottering about though he kept looking at his watch and dropping hints about them having to go soon. It was well into the afternoon when the Scotts arrived back and to her complete dismay Chrisann saw that Ullin accompanied them.

Jean came up to Chrisann to say that Ullin had requested she have a meal with him at Dykehill. "I'm just going up to prepare it now," nodded Jean, trying not to appear too curious about Raymond. Chrisann automatically introduced him, explained that he had slept the night in the living-room, and wondered desperately how she was going to get out of dining with Ullin.

But Raymond settled the matter by rubbing his hands together and saying, "Sounds good, I'm starving, it must be all this fresh air." Jean went off and Ullin strode over with that lithe easy tread Chrisann knew so well. He was wearing a tweed-look fisherman's jersey and brown cords tucked into wellington boots and he looked so big and husky and so devastatingly handsome she felt again that insane desire to touch him.

"Jean tells me that you have accepted my invitation to dine with me," he said politely, but he was looking at Raymond and Chrisann sensed his suspicion. The old anger rose up in her. What right had he to send Jean to issue an invitation that should have come from him? He was so ill-mannered he had just assumed she would accept humbly and be grateful to him for the honour of his company. Why did he want to dine with her anyway? What were his reasons for pestering her all the time when he had made it quite plain last night it wouldn't matter to him if he never saw her again. "I was coming to ask you myself but Jean got to you first," he explained and it was as if he had read her thoughts. "If I had known you had company I wouldn't have intruded."

Raymond held out his hand and said pleasantly, "How do you do, old man; since Chrisann doesn't look like doing the honours I'll introduce myself – Raymond Carstairs. I'm the chap who takes pretty pictures of pretty girls – and this one," he put an arm intimately round Chrisann's shoulders, "is one of my favourite models if not *the* favourite. I arrived on her last night never expecting to find myself all alone with her on a Hebridean island."

Chrisann squirmed as Ullin's jaw tightened. Rather tersely he told Raymond his name and curtly requesting that they follow him he strode quickly away.

Raymond looked after him and said thoughtfully, "I'm beginning to see why you extended your stay here, Chrisann, the chap has that animal appeal that some women find irresistible. It's perhaps a good job I came to stop you from doing anything foolish; can't have you falling for a fisherman, can we?"

She was too apprehensive about everything to even begin to argue with Raymond or to correct his assumptions about Ullin and with trailing footsteps she walked with him over the winding paths to Dykehill where Jean was busy in the kitchen and Ullin was employed in lighting the fire in the living-room. In no time the meal was ready and after serving it Jean hurried away.

"Marvellous cooks these island women," commented Raymond, appreciatively eyeing the contents of his plate. "I wouldn't mind someone like Jean working for me. A chap gets pretty tired dining out all the time. It would be nice to come home at night to some good old home cooking."

"I don't think Jean's family will let her go at any price," said Ullin pleasantly and Raymond's rather serious face broke into a smile.

"Good, very good, MacBeth. I had heard you island people have a droll sense of humour – rather an interesting name you have there – Ullin MacBeth wasn't it? No relation to the Lord Ullin of the poem?"

Ullin's eyes glinted with sardonic amusement as he shook his head. Chrisann kept her eyes glued on her plate. She had no appetite and picked at the delicious cheese soufflé Jean had prepared so carefully. Raymond was going on, talking all the time he was attacking his food.

"I've got this feeling I've seen you somewhere before, MacBeth, just pure fancy of course, you're shut away from it all on the islands. Still – oddest notion I've seen you around – I say, this soufflé is damned good, no more for the asking, I suppose?"

Chrisann rose and went to the oven, lingering there as she thought of Raymond's words. It was quite likely that he had seen Ullin around, his job took him all over the place; he was quite often in Glasgow and Edinburgh – Edinburgh – the North British hotel. Ullin had stayed there with Claire and Raymond had been doing a lot of photography in the Scottish capital last year using the tattoo as background for his work. . . .

"Come on, Chrisann." Raymond's imperative tones brought her out of her reverie. Automatically she spooned food onto his plate and he patted her hand approvingly. "Good girl, must feed your man, eh?" he leaned across to Ullin confidentially. "Beautiful girl, eh, MacBeth? Mind you, she's let herself go a bit since coming out to the wilds. All this fresh air has gone to her head but we'll soon rectify that. A bit of a work load ahead of her, I'm afraid, but after that it's the sun for her and me – the south of France or wherever she fancies. It will do her good to have a real holiday – this camping lark was just another of her whims – pass the butter, there's a good chap."

Chrisann bit back the arguments rising up inside her. When Raymond was like this it was no use talking to him.

When the meal was over they moved into the living-room for drinks. "Damned good whisky this, MacBeth," said Raymond appreciatively. He glanced round the room. "Nice little place you have here, wouldn't mind something like it for weekends and holidays. Must be hellish in the winter though, nothing to do but twiddle your thumbs; I'd go mad with boredom."

"Winter is often our busiest time." Ullin's tones were level and it was obvious that he wasn't going to give anything away about himself. "The beasts don't go into hibernation, you know, they must be fed and looked after."

"Quite, but I didn't mean that. Night life and the like, can't get much of that out here." He put down his glass. "Still, I've enjoyed your hospitality; I must say you Scots are a good-hearted lot once you burrow under the surface." He rubbed his hands together and looked at Chrisann who hadn't uttered a word in the last ten minutes. "Come on then, darling, I'll go down and get my bag and you can collect your things."

Chrisann's heart thudded. She didn't want to go with Raymond, on the other hand she didn't want to make her protests in front of Ullin in case he imagined for one moment she wanted to stay on Ronnach because of him.

Raymond went off and immediately Ullin whirled Chrisann round to face him, his hand on her arm like a steel clamp. "Just what the hell do you think you're playing at?" he demanded, his eyes as hard as flint. "First you run away from Strathullin, now I find you've spent the night with Carstairs. Don't you have any sense of decency in you at all? Can you imagine what folks around here will have to say when talk like that leaks out?"

"I don't give a damn what people will say!" she cried wildly and unthinkingly. "Because I won't be here to let it worry me!"

"That's right, run away!" he lashed out, his fingers tightening on her arm. "Your kind of morals don't quite fit in here, city girl."

"Don't tell me you're jealous?" she cried. "I'm not one of your loyal subjects; I don't bend over backwards to give you the only thing you've wanted from me ever since I came here! Does it annoy you to think that a lesser mortal might have succeeded where you so miserably failed!"

His face was livid in those moments, his white teeth clenched as he ground out contemptuously, "I could have taken you any time I wanted, city girl, and damned fine you know it! You've panted after me with such vigour you were quite exhausted when the chase finally ended in the bedroom, so much so you switched off when you found the trail had grown so hot you had to get off before you got more than your toes burned. Carstairs must be quite something if he got anywhere with you! What did he do? Tie you to the bedpost!"

"You're a despicable boorish brute," she sobbed weakly. "And your mind is as pitifully corrupt as your desires. I've never hated any man as I hate you and I pray I'll never have the misfortune to set eyes on you again."

"Your prayers have just been answered," he gritted harshly and abruptly released her arm. She flew from him, over the fields and onto the road. She thought she was going to faint, her heart was pounding madly in her breast. Stopping for breath she glanced up and saw on the brow of the hill a tall, lithe figure whose hair was a crown of gold against the blue sky. His outline blurred and angrily she brushed the tears from her eyes as she began to run once more. All her things were in Jean's house but she couldn't face anyone just then and she ran past the house to the shore.

Raymond was waiting beside the boat manned by Dave, a dark-bearded young man who spent his time fishing on the stretch of water between Mull and Ronnach. "Come on, darling," said Raymond as she panted up. "I was lucky to catch this chap and if we don't get a move on we'll miss the ferry at Craignure."

Dave gallantly took Chrisann's arm as she lowered herself onto a thwart. Turning she saw Jean hanging out clothes at the back of the house. She wanted to shout a farewell for she had grown very fond of the Scott family – with a small strangled sob she looked away. She didn't want to see Ronnach growing further and further away. Dejectedly she clasped her arms over her breasts as if to hug warmth to herself and her hands rasped over the rough material of the denim jacket Ullin had given her to protect her clothes when she had been helping with the sheep. With an impulsive movement she snatched it off and stuffed it under the thwart. Dressed only in jeans and her pink T-shirt she shivered as a cold wind skittered over the waves.

"Best put your jacket back on," nodded Dave. "It's cold out on the water."

"The chap is right, Chrisann," frowned Raymond, rubbing at a patch of oil on his otherwise immaculate trousers. "You'll catch your death and that's no good to anyone. Haven't you anything else to wear? Where are all your things?"

But she didn't answer. Lowering her head she stole a glance at Ronnach through the veil of her long lashes. She didn't want to look but the island was like a magnet, forcing her to look against her will. It was like a green and gold jewel lying on the sun-dappled blue water. The smoke from Jean's chimney spiralled up into the sky – and beyond that she saw a wisping opalescent quiver of mist curling up from the hollows of emerald fields: the smoke from Ullin's fire. The memory of his face contorted in anger came to her. She clasped her hands together and shivered again. Don't look back, she pleaded with herself desperately but time and again, as the oars slapped rhythmically and the waves pulsated against the bow, she turned her head to watch the dream that was Ronnach fading into the pearly distance.

Chapter Nine

Chrisann curled up in the back seat of the car. She felt exhausted, her limbs were leaden, her eyes so heavy she felt she wanted to close them and sleep forever. But the emotions that bubbled in her heart wouldn't let her rest. She ached, with misery, with hurt – but most of all with anger. Raymond did all the talking. Sitting behind the wheel, his back straight, his face animated, he talked for most of the journey to Craignure. When he realized he was getting no response he demanded peevishly, "For heaven's sake, Chrisann, what *is* the matter with you? It's that fellow back there isn't it? MacBeth. If you ask me I just came in the nick of time. You simply can't allow yourself to moon over a chap like that. Take it from me, it's just a holiday romance. I've had them myself you know, felt quite sick over some of them—"

"Oh, do be quiet, Raymond. I've got a headache."

"And so have I, damn you! I didn't just come here at Anthony's bidding, you know, I came because I love you and that in itself is about one of the worst headaches I've ever known. You don't believe me, do you? Think I'll get over it like—"

"All the others," she finished wearily. "You will, Raymond, believe me, you will."

"Chrisann—"

"Raymond," she said warningly. "That's enough. Just – don't let's talk about it."

She sat up and leaning over the passenger seat, pulled down the vanity flap to peer in the mirror. "Oh, look at me! I don't even have a comb, and my face is streaked with dust."

"Here, use mine." He pulled a comb from his pocket and handed it over.

"You *are* a mess," he scolded softly. "And you smell of TCP. What on earth is it?"

"Sheep dip."

"Sheep dip!"

"Yes, I was helping out at the dipping last week – and don't you dare laugh! I enjoyed it, it was hard work but fun – and – and . . ."

"Here." He waved his white hanky at her like a flag. "Blow your nose. You'll feel better when you've had a night's sleep. By the way, I'll phone the Central from Oban and book us a first class sleeper."

"Make that two," she said with a faint smile, then added, "have you got a cigarette?"

"But, you stopped that ages ago."

"As from now I've started again."

She sat in the back seat, puffing furiously at the king-sized filter tip he handed over but it made her cough and feel sick. Crushing it out in the ashtray she leaned back and listlessly watched the scenery flashing past. The Sound of Mull was a vivid blue, the hills of Morvern a hazy purple. It was beautiful but she had no eye for any of it. All her enthusiasm had sapped away leaving her drained.

After the quiet of Ronnach, the journey over on the boat to Oban was noisy and smelly with car exhaust fumes. Raymond took her along to the saloon where he ordered tea and pancakes but she only sipped at the tea and pecked at the edge of a pancake. People laughed, talked too loudly, jostled. At Oban she experienced terrible pangs of guilt remembering her promises to her parents and just as Raymond was about to deliver the car back to the car hirers the realization came to her that there was no earthly reason why she couldn't go and spend at least one night at home.

"I'm going to see my mum and dad, Raymond," she stated flatly. "You can go on ahead of me to London. I'll catch up with you tomorrow."

"Oh no you don't." He sounded determined. "I'm not letting you out of my sight again. Any reason why I can't come and meet your parents?"

"None at all, if you don't mind sleeping in a tiny box of a room."

"Darling, I'm so tired I could sleep in a box. Show me the way to your home," he trilled and she had to smile. He was being nice to her, more considerate than the Raymond she was used to. He really was fond of her and not as thick-skinned as he made out.

She introduced him to her parents, going through all the usual formalities, the niceties. Mr and Mrs McNeil were delighted at the intrusion and not in the least put out by the unexpected arrival of Raymond onto the scene. Chrisann felt her heart twisting over with love for them for she realized that they were willing to put up with anything or anyone just for the privilege of having their daughter with them.

Mr McNeil took Raymond off to the sitting-room and Chrisann stood smiling at her mother in the hall.

"He's a very nice young man," said Mrs McNeil though there was an expression of bemusement in her dark eyes. "Hardly your type I would have thought, but then, we know so little about you now, what sort of friends you have in London. I suppose we aren't really qualified to know what your type is."

Chrisann put her arm round her mother's slim shoulders.

"Raymond's a rogue, a likeable one but a rogue. He's not my type and never was."

"But—"

"I know, he told you he was my fiancé – he isn't, it was a trick to find out where I was."

"Oh, Chrisann, I'm so sorry."

"Oh, Mum, don't say another word about it. Let's just enjoy our time together. You and I could go shopping tomorrow. I haven't a thing to wear, also I must buy some make-up."

Mrs McNeil laughed. "You do look rather – how could I put it – unmodellish. What have you been doing, darling? You look well, far better than the last time I saw you, but you *smell* very strange and what on earth has happened to all your things?"

Chrisann's eyes clouded. "I'll explain sometime. Right now all I want is a bath and bed."

"Chrisann, you *look* better but that sparkle I heard in your voice when you phoned me from Ronnach, has gone. I know you won't tell me right away what troubles you but – has it something to do with the Mr MacBeth you spoke about?"

Chrisann took a deep breath. "Yes, Mum, but it's over now and I don't want ever to rake any of it up. I'm going upstairs now to have a bath. I shan't want anything to eat."

"But, Chrisann, you should, you're far too thin—"

"Good-night, Mum, see you in the morning."

She went up to her room and stood looking round at the familiar things she had known since childhood yet the sight of them brought her no comfort, instead they only served to heighten her awareness of things that were gone never to return: childhood; the eager searching teenage years; the times she should have spent with her parents but hadn't. She had always been too busy pursuing her career to give much thought to anything else. Ullin had sharply pointed that fact out to her and guilt had made her quickly change the subject. A sense of incredible loneliness washed over her and she passed a weary hand over her eyes and listlessly went to run her bath only to find her mother in the bathroom. She had run a steaming perfumed bath and was laying big fluffy clean towels over the hot rail. "Oh Mum, you shouldn't," protested Chrisann. "I'm perfectly capable of seeing to such things myself."

"I know, and it isn't often I get the chance to spoil you and really, dear, I just had to make sure you got rid of that awful aroma of sheep dip."

They both laughed and impulsively Chrisann put her arms round her mother and hugged her tightly as she said, "I've spent far too much time away from you and Dad. In future you'll be seeing much more of me, I really mean that."

Mrs McNeil's pleasant face grew serious. "I wish you did, Chrisann, it would be lovely to really get to know you again. Your father and I have always been proud of you and delighted at your success – yet because of it we've missed sharing in your life."

"Oh, Mum, I'm sorry," cried Chrisann. "I really will try to make it up to you."

Her mother turned at the door and said, "All we really want is for you to be happy – and at the moment you're not though I'm not going to ask you why. I've a feeling it will all come out in the wash anyway."

The door closed softly and Chrisann undressed and got into the bath to wonder if her mother's words would come true and it would 'All come out in the wash'. But angrily she shook off such notions. Ullin MacBeth was bad news, he was a philanderer, a conceited unmannerly one at that. He accused her of creating a bad reputation for herself when he himself had behaved shockingly, chasing her relentlessly, trying to seduce her at every turn and in his fury at having failed, mustering the nerve to rant and rave at her like a madman, to hurl abuse and accusations at her that were totally unwarranted.

Glancing at her arm she saw the red marks left by his brutally powerful fingers and rage gripped her afresh. How dare he hurt her like that? How dare he think he had the right to touch her at all – to kiss her and caress her as if she was his property. . . . The remembrance of the possessive pressure of his lips claiming hers was so strong that she shut her eyes as if to shut out the memories – but she knew that she could never shut him from her mind. She hated him yet her physical need for him was such that she couldn't stop imagining what ecstasy there would be in the final surrender to his supremely masculine body. . . .

"Stop it, stop it," she protested aloud. "He belongs to Claire. . . ." She stuffed her fist against her mouth. Oh yes, how he belonged to Claire! And she obviously belonged to him. She had made that plain enough right from the start.

As she was going across the hall she heard Raymond coming upstairs and hastily she dived into her room knowing that if he saw her he would try to kiss her and she couldn't take any more emotional wrangles in her present frame of mind.

Although she was exhausted she couldn't sleep. The house was silent when she slipped out of bed and padded over to the window. The peace of night lay over the fishing port like a soft dark blanket. The waters of the Firth of Lorne were midnight blue velvet flecked with silver from the guide lights of fishing boats . . . and far far in the distance the ethereal shadow of Mull lay against the star-studded horizon. It was a mere flimsy shape, slightly darker than the dark horizon and it was only because she knew it was there that she could make it out at all.

She shivered in the cool air of night and folded her arms across her breasts. She thought about Kirsty and Mary, Colin Mor and Jean, Bob and Jamie. . . . She had left her bicycle and her camping things at the Scotts' house. She ought to go back for them; it would be a good excuse to see them all again. . . . Almost before the idea had gelled she drew back from the window – she couldn't go back; she mustn't ever go back. Miserably she went back to bed only to sleep fitfully, a sleep that was full of strange dreams, of yearnings and frustrations.

"Darling, you look *awful!*" was Raymond's greeting when she came down to breakfast. "Hardly slept at all from the look of you. Not still hankering after that MacBeth chap I hope."

"Oh for heaven's sake, do be quiet!" she snapped. "You talk far too much."

"Pardon me for living," he returned sulkily. "I promise I won't say another word for the rest of the day."

It was an impossible promise of course. After Mr McNeil went off to the shop Raymond took Chrisann and her mother round Oban, talking all the time, advising Chrisann on the kind of clothes he thought would suit her, enthusiastically exclaiming over her when she emerged from one store, wearing a well-cut white linen trouser suit.

"He really is rather sweet," Chrisann's mother whispered and Chrisann smiled and agreed even while her eyes gazed hungrily at the shadowed drift of the Mull hills on the distant horizon. She couldn't bear it, to look and remember a man called Ullin who said things with his lips and lied to her with his deeds, and before the morning was over she got her mother alone and took her hands.

"Mum, I'm not waiting till tonight to go back to London, I'm going after we've had a bite of lunch. . . . I'll – I'll be back as soon as I can get away again."

The hurt in her mother's eyes made her shiver with guilt. "Very well, Chrisann," said Mrs McNeil quietly. "Dad will be disappointed, he was looking forward to seeing you at tea time – but you must do what you want of course."

After lunch, at the station, she squeezed her daughter's hand. "My darling little girl," she whispered. "How I wish you were closer to us." The goodbyes were said and it was only when Chrisann was on the train that her mother's words really hit home. Had they meant closer in relation to distance – or closer in spirit?

The wheels of the train clattered the miles away, beating a tattoo inside her head till very soon they formed a rhythm: Ullin MacBeth, Ullin MacBeth, Ullin MacBeth. Raymond was rather quiet beside her and to get away from her own thoughts she began to chatter too brightly about all the things that were relevant to them both but he just listened without comment and when she paused for breath he said dryly, "You're trying too hard, my sweet. Don't use me as a shock absorber, please. I love you very much but I'm far too selfish and jealous to try and soothe your feelings over another man." Broodingly he studied her face. "I must say, I've never known you behave like this over a man – and the fact that he's just an ordinary sort of fellow doesn't make things any easier. Surely a girl like you ought to be on the lookout for a steady sort, one with a bit of style, a good profession, a bit of lolly to set you up in the manner you are accustomed to – a chap like myself for instance."

She sat back and despite herself couldn't suppress a smile. "Raymond, you are a fool, but a darling just the same. Top marks for trying but you're wrong about Ullin, he isn't in the least ordinary, the very opposite, in fact. However, I don't want to discuss him right now so please leave me alone. I want to close my eyes, I – I didn't get much sleep last night."

She closed her eyes but didn't sleep. All she could think about was Ronnach and a sturdy grey house set against a green hillside. The miles flew past as quickly as the pictures flashing through her mind: pictures of blue seas; of Staffa; of swimming; of white sands and breathless sunsets; of Ullin. Ullin in firelight; in sunlight; in misted rain; in dreams. A blond giant whose deep voice spoke honeyed words in her ears; whose strong brown arms promised undreamed of delights; whose lips lifted her to heights of glory and whose deeds toppled her into a pit of hopeless despair.

Many weary hours later she stood on the seething platform of Euston station and now Ronnach really was a dream. Dazed and bewildered she allowed Raymond to lead her through the busy streets. Soon they were in a taxi speeding through the night life of London. The bright lights flashed past; anonymous dark figures seemed pasted against the background of glitter. It was raining slightly, the pavements shone, reflecting the varied hues of neon signs, the lights of traffic were all around her. Closing her eyes she tried to conjure the scents of the Hebrides but it was useless and she panicked a little and opened her eyes, surprised to discover they were now in the quieter territory of Kensington. Elegant buildings loomed and it was all so familiar she felt she might never have been away. The noise of the city was muffled but still there, in the near vicinity, reminding her that even at night London throbbed with life.

At the door of her flat Raymond leaned forward and kissed her lightly on the cheek. "See you in the morning." He sounded weary.

"Yes. . . . Raymond, thank you for everything. I'm afraid I've been a bit of a bitch to you since Saturday. . . ." She paused. On Saturday she had still been on Ronnach, feeling the kiss of the sun on her face, savouring Ullin's kisses on her lips . . . another world – gone from her. "I'm sorry, Raymond, you really are quite a darling, you know."

"I know." It was a jocular remark without humour. He touched her face briefly. "Have a good night, darling, you must have your beauty sleep."

"Yes," she said dully and turning the key in the lock she went inside. It was just as she had left it though dustier, slightly neglected-looking. She trod softly over the beige-coloured carpet, touching things: the white wool chairs; the smoke-blue glass of the occasional tables; the wall units with their expensive array of Capo di Monte ornaments. She had taken such a delight in her flat; it had been her haven when things had got on top of her. Now it seemed empty and sad, echoing a past way of life which now seemed pointless.

She sank down on a pile of fun cushions and folded her arms over her breasts. She was back where she belonged. All that was familiar in her life was here – in London – but she couldn't stop the thoughts that crowded in on her. All that was sweet and warm and peaceful was back in the dream that was Ronnach – and so too were all the treacherous temptations invoked in her by a man called Ullin.

Chapter Ten

During the following week Chrisann threw herself into her job with such energetic devotion that, after the initial approval, those who worked close with her, began to grow alarmed. Each night she went home and fell exhausted into bed, each morning she dragged herself wearily from bed, and forced herself into another strenuous day during which she hardly ate or rested.

"Chrisann," Raymond faced her one day, his face tense, "this will have to stop. You can't go on like this, you'll kill yourself."

"You wanted it," she told him tiredly. "You all wanted it. Wasn't that the reason you followed me to Ronnach – chased me up – wouldn't let go? Well, you're getting what you so obviously desired. I'm working, Raymond, like hell I'm working so stop complaining."

Anthony was more brutal. "Chrisann," his lips were very tight, "what, I may ask, has gotten into you? First you run away and then you come back like a dervish. I wanted you to clear your commitments but I don't want this! You're washed out, darling. You look awful. I think the best thing for us all would be if you went home and rested for a couple of days."

She looked at him with contempt. "Well, thanks a lot, Anthony. It's just what I might have expected from you of course. It's all business with you, isn't it? People are just machines to you. Their feelings don't come into it."

His podgy hand came out to her but she cringed away as he said, "Feelings don't count in my book. You have to be strong for all this, darling, you ought to know that by now. Let personal life enter in and the strain soon starts to show. Go home and catch up on your beauty sleep – from the look of you, you need it."

With trailing steps she arrived at her flat, feeling desolate and rejected. The sun was shining in a blue sky and she caught herself thinking, if it's like this in Scotland Ronnach will be golden, the sea will be like a sapphire with the Treshnish Isles scattered on it like beautiful jewels. . . . She jumped out of her reverie with a startled gasp for pinned on her door was a little bunch of heather. She stared at it and her heart bounded so fast she felt the beat of it deep inside her head. It wasn't heather, it was a sprig of Crowberry, the clan plant of the MacBeths. The tiny narrow leaves were fresh and green; purple-black berries clung to the stem.

"Some day I'll fetch you a sprig of Crowberry from the mountains." Ullin's promise came back to her as if he was standing beside her saying it. All the breath seemed to be squeezing out of her lungs. He was here! Ullin was here! She looked round quickly as if expecting him to walk out from the shadows. He had been here. The wild mountain plant was still fresh and dewy. She tried to get breath and while she struggled she stood with her brow against the doorpost, her glorious black hair falling like a curtain over her face.

After a while she straightened her aching shoulders and turning the key in the door she went inside. Removing her claret-red velvet jacket she let it trail along the floor behind her as she made her way to the bedroom where she changed out of her white satin blouse and black cord skirt and into her favourite silk, multicoloured kaftan, which she used for lounging. A drink! She needed a drink, something strong to steady her and help her gather her thoughts together.

Going to the drinks cabinet in the lounge she poured herself a good measure of brandy and stood for a moment warming it in her hands. "Make that two." The deep cultured voice coming from the depths of the swivel armchair by the window made her jump so violently she slopped some of the brandy onto the polished surface of the drinks cabinet. Slowly she turned. The back of the chair was to her, the sun poured over a head of bright hair, hair the colour of ripe wheat. The chair swung round and a pair of vivid blue eyes regarded her in triumphant amusement. All the strength that was left in her flowed and bubbled, channelling upwards in a tide of violent outrage.

"How did you get in here?" she cried, her trembling hands clutching the glass so tightly she thought it would snap. "Get out, get out of my house this very minute or I'll call the police."

"Now, now." He was pulling himself to his feet, coming towards her, big, looming, somehow terrifying even though his voice was modulated, in control. "That's no way to speak to someone who took you in and gave you food and shelter."

She backed away from him. "Don't you dare touch me, you – you brute! Tell me, tell me how you got into my home! I want to know, now, this minute or I'll scream the place down."

"This." He whipped a photograph from an inner pocket and held it up. It was a picture of her.

"How did you get that?" Her voice had lowered to a horrified whisper. "Where did you get it?"

"Your mother gave it to me, together with a bit of history concerning your uncle Theadore who I believe is in Canada at the moment. I showed the picture to the caretaker downstairs, a picture of my favourite niece. I believe you have spoken very highly of your uncle to the caretaker. When I told him that I had just arrived from Canada on a flying visit he seemed very impressed. Even so he was a bit cautious; however, a few of the old greenbacks soon settled his mind." He grinned. "Am I not going to get a kiss of welcome from my favourite niece?"

"You're despicable, a liar and a cheat!" she lashed out at him. "What right have you got to go and see my parents? Inveigle your way in here! How could Mum be taken in by you? But I almost forgot, that deadly charm of yours! Well, it won't work now, Ullin MacBeth! Get out of here! I don't want to see you or hear from you again!"

"Why did you run away, Chrisann?" he asked, as if she hadn't spoken. "At first I thought it might be that there was something between you and Raymond after all but when I calmed down a bit I soon realized that an assumption like that was too stupid for words. A friend Raymond may be but a sweetheart he is not. Was it fear that made you flee from me? Fear that at last your heart has caught up with you? Was it, Chrisann, tell me, I really would like to know."

His voice was so harsh and cold she felt a wave of faintness washing over her, robbing her of the breath to answer. She shook her head, her hair tumbling over her face, hiding it.

"You don't look well, Chrisann," his voice was softer now. "All that lovely colour you had on Ronnach has gone. Working too hard, eh? Trying to forget, trying to fool yourself into the belief that all that matters to you is your job. Running away from the truth, from the things your heart is trying to tell you but which your foolish mind won't listen to."

Slowly she looked up, her violet eyes huge in her white strained face. "Don't you dare call me a fool! You've said it once too often! You are what I thought you were when first I met you: a barbarian; a bully – a – a womanizer who thinks that all women ought to swoon at your feet. You're living in the past, Mr MacBeth. You've shut yourself away from civilization for too long."

Roughly he caught her wrists. She arched her body and kicked out at him but he merely laughed and held on. "You talk in riddles, my lovely darling. Why don't you give in? You will in the end. I'm not letting you go again. Stop fighting with yourself; you belong to me, you've belonged to me since the first moment I saw you on the hill."

"Let me go!" she yelled breathlessly. "You've got it wrong, Mr Macbeth, I'm not in the queue! Don't you know I loathe you! Or are you so smug and conceited you can't believe any woman could possibly resist you! I wonder you had the nerve to come here like this but then you have the nerve for anything. And why should you assume there's nothing between Raymond and me? He at least has manners. . . ."

Ullin's grip moved painfully to her shoulders and his blue eyes bored into hers. "Are you trying to drive me crazy by such hints?" he gritted harshly. "*Is* there some sort of relationship between you and Carstairs?"

She shrugged as nonchalantly as she could. "What if there is? At least he's faithful in his own way. At least he doesn't go off on hot pursuit of one girl while another learns she might be carrying his child!"

"Just what do you mean by that?" Ullin's voice was dangerously calm and in a rush of panic Chrisann repeated the things Claire had said to her on the night of the reception at Strathullin House.

"Idiot!" he clipped, his face as white as hers. "Claire went to the doctor, yes, but only to see about a grumbling appendix. It was just another of her vindictive little schemes to get you out of the way and you fell for it. Do you honestly believe I would give such a gold digger a chance to get her hooks into me? Do you?"

"But – all these hints she dropped about you and she together. . . ."

"She saw you as a threat and set about getting rid of you," he said harshly then added with a bitter laugh, "oh I'm not denying that I find her attractive! I'm not blind! I took what she readily offered me. I'm no monk, believe me. But when I saw she meant business I began to avoid her like the plague only the more I ran the faster she came after me. She had no intention of letting go without putting up a fight. She was there at every turn. She even inveigled her way into Dykehill and began using Kirsty's things, always having some excuse to bathe and parade about in skimpy clothing. Oh, I'm not saying I wasn't tempted, I was, but I was damned if she was going to get the better of me. Does that satisfy you?"

"I'm sorry," she faltered, "I should never have believed all these things yet I couldn't help it. You've been so hurtful and beastly to me ever since we met I was in a muddle over everything. I don't understand so many things; I don't know why you chased me away from Strathullin House—"

"Chased you?" he asked incredulously.

"Yes, chased me, with your harsh words, your – your contempt. Just because I wouldn't let you have your own way. . . ."

His eyes narrowed to ice blue chips, "Haven't we discussed all this before?" he snapped shortly. "Why won't you be honest with yourself? That night at Strathullin you wanted me as much as I wanted you. I am very much flesh and blood, Chrisann, you drove me to the brink—"

"*I* drove you?" she cried in disbelief. "You pursued me like a – like a mad, lust-filled dog! You were there at every turn, tormenting me, teasing me, mocking me. Oh, I'll admit you have that certain magnetic allure that some women might find hard to resist—"

"*Some* women? But not you? Do you really expect me to believe that?" His voice was dangerously level, his vice like hold tightened on her arm, he thrust his face close to hers till his lips were just inches away. In terror she strained her head back only to feel the fingers of his free hand running through the silken threads of her hair.

"All right," she whimpered, "I find you hard to resist but that doesn't stop me hating you nor does it help me to understand you. I can't understand a man who pushes me off one minute and the next coolly invites me to have a meal with him as if nothing had happened."

"Nothing did happen," he said, and his voice was terrifyingly calm. "And I came after you because I was worried about you being on the island on your own—"

"You left it long enough," she gasped, awed by his utter audacity.

"Yes, I admit that," he acceded. "To be frank I had to wait till I cooled down enough to feel guilty at the things I said. By way of apology I thought it would be a good idea to make things up over a meal."

"I see," she squeezed out, wishing she could stop herself from breathing so quickly. "I'm glad you at last felt human enough to climb down off your pedestal to actually want to apologize to a mere female. As to being worried about me being alone on the island – you didn't suffer from any such sense of anxiety when you left me alone at Dykehill on the night of the storm—"

"What gave you that idea?" he cut in brusquely.

"Claire told me – she said you had spent the night at Sam's cottage."

He threw back his head and laughed derisively. "She *has* been busy yet in a way she's right about everything she says though she has a way of twisting the truth that borders on the brilliant. I didn't go running off to Sam's because of you. When I went out that night to look at your tent I met him and he told me that one of the cows was having a difficult time calving so as soon as I saw you safely tucked in bed I went out to give Sam a hand. It was early in the morning when I got back and rather than go up to bed I spent a few hours on the living-room couch." His eyes gleamed with amusement. "You dear little idiot. Is that why you've been going on about my precious reputation? Did you honestly believe I would go running off with my tail between my legs because I was afraid that people would think I had lured you out of the storm to share my bed?"

She couldn't speak. All her anger had evaporated to be replaced by an emotion so deep and raw it seeped through all the defences she had built up against him. Bullying and savagery she could fight – but not tenderness – and it was there . . . in his voice . . . his eyes . . . in the gentle coaxing pressure of his hand on the back of her head.

"Don't, please don't," she gasped out as his lips came closer and closer. "I know you think I'm just a glamour girl with very few brains. You laughed at my camping efforts, you took a delight in making me feel a fool—"

"Hush," he cut in softly. "I admired you for doing the camping bit – at least you tried. You got dirty and wet and you smelled of sheep dip but you didn't mind and you enjoyed it all. Oh, Chrisann, you're so very very beautiful."

She felt herself drowning in wave upon wave of the

most exquisite joy she had ever known. He didn't care about Claire, he cared about her, cared enough to come to London to seek her out. . . . His arms enclosed her, he was kissing her eyes, her nose, her throat. She clung to him without shame or fear, a joyous wonder in her as the realization that she loved him engulfed her, carried her away in an all-consuming wave of emotion. She could feel the thudding of his heart beating into her, merging with her own till it seemed they shared the same throbbing life force.

"Chrisann, I've got so much to say to you. . . ." His voice was low and husky and rather shaky.

"I love you, Ullin," she whispered, savouring his name on her lips. "My life was very well regulated until we met; now everything is upside down – and it's wonderful."

He kissed her, a kiss of fire that sent the blood surging through her veins like the swell of the Atlantic Ocean beating to the shore. His hands slid over the silk of her kaftan, mobile expert hands that were so supremely confident; her legs trembled as an overpowering shaft of longing shot through her.

"I loved the feel of you in angora – but I think . . . silk . . . is even nicer," he murmured and his kisses became deeper, his body harder, his exploring hands more and more urgent. But quite suddenly he drew away from her, a flush on his bronzed face. He began to pace and she sensed the need in him. Restlessly he straightened his tie and for the first time she noticed his clothes: immaculate dark slacks, a well-cut cream wool sport's jacket set off by a pale blue shirt. He was so unlike the casually-dressed Ullin of Ronnach, yet, he looked right in such garb and so devastatingly handsome her heart turned over and she ached to be once again in the protective embrace of his strong arms.

"Chrisann – could you . . . after all this . . . bear to live in the country?" The question was curt, anxious.

Her heart beat quickly. "I – I've thought of nowhere else but Mull and Ronnach since coming back here."

"Thinking and doing are entirely different affairs. You live a very glamorous existence here – could you honestly exchange it all for the quiet of a Hebridean island?"

She knew what he was thinking. His wife had loathed living in the country and he wasn't going to repeat an episode in his life which had failed so drastically. "I've pined for the Hebrides more than you can ever know," she told him seriously. "I'm not a silly child, Ullin, this has been wonderful but I have played it out. I'm tired, Ullin, I'm tired of it all."

"Then – will you marry me, my darling? Under all my barbaric ways I'm rather old-fashioned. I discussed all this with your parents – asked their permission to ask you; they were delighted – after all I suppose I'm quite a catch for a beautiful successful girl who can have her pick of any man she chooses. I warn you though, before you answer – I want it understood that if you say yes you must look upon me as the breadwinner. You aren't exactly on the breadline, are you?"

"No, I'm not," she laughed happily. "In fact I've made quite a tidy little fortune over the years and have a good accountant who made me invest it wisely. But we'll leave it to grow nice and fat – as far as I'm concerned when we are married you will be the provider, though on occasion you might allow me to help with the animals."

"Then – it's settled." His blue gaze held hers as he drew out a small red box and instructing her to hold out her hand he slipped an engagement ring onto her slim finger. It was an amethyst clasped by two gold horseshoes in a platinum setting. A lump rose in her throat. "My birthstone," she said softly. "How did you know?"

"Your father, of course, where else would I buy your ring but from the best jeweller's in Oban?"

"Are my parents pleased?" she heard herself saying through a daze of happiness. "Is Kirsty?"

"The last time I saw them they were all doing a joyful war dance in and out of McCaig's Folly."

She shouted with merriment and he crushed her into his arms. She lay against him, feeling the heat of his body pulsing into her, his hands caressing her hair, hearing him say, "I want us to be married quickly, tomorrow wouldn't be too soon, but, as I've been married before I will have to settle for a wait of about six weeks. The marriage notices must be submitted right away – at Oban if you want the wedding there – you can also decide if it's to be church or registry. I know women like all the fuss of a church do and of course your mother will want her daughter—"

"Hold on, you go too fast for me, give me time to get used to the idea."

"No time I'm afraid, my darling, this isn't an idea, it's pure fact – besides, if we don't marry quickly I can't promise to go on behaving myself. I'm losing sleep thinking about you in my arms. Will you come back with me now? We must get these notices into the registrar."

She thought briefly about her job. Anthony couldn't have foreseen any of this but he had given her time off when she most needed it and she blessed him for it.

"What will Carstairs say?" Ullin's voice broke into her thoughts.

She caught him and kissed him. "What can he say? I never promised him anything. I like him as a friend but that's all." She giggled. "And just in case you still have doubts – the night he came to Ronnach he slept in my camp bed in the living-room and I slept in Mary's room as usual."

"I think in my heart I knew that. It was just the idea – of you and him—"

"What about you and Claire?" she cut in rather sharply. "That evening you had dinner with her, for instance?"

"That was all it was," he said softly. "Dinner, drinks, a friendly chat. No doubt she won't be pleased when she hears about us but that can't be helped."

"You wanted Stonehurst very badly," she pointed out.

"Can't win them all," he said into her ear. "I've given up the idea of owning Stonehurst. Knowing Claire she'll make it without me."

"If I hadn't come along you – you might have ended up with Stonehurst . . . and Claire," she said faintly.

"You did come along – and that's an end to the matter." His voice was low and as his mouth came down on hers he swept away all her fears on a tide of sensuous delight.

The next few weeks went past in a whirl. She divided her time between London and Oban. Her mother came to spend a few days in London and they shopped for the trousseau in a rash, exciting spending spree. Mrs McNeil was almost as excited as her daughter about the forthcoming marriage and Chrisann, looking at her mother's happy, sweet face, felt this was what she had missed during her busy years as a fashion model. The bond had been in danger of breaking but now they made up for all the lost time. Girlfriends, trendy, eager, fashion-conscious, gave Chrisann all sorts of advice about the sort of dress she ought to wear for her marriage but in the end it was Chrisann and her mother who chose it together, an elegant creation in cream silk with a figure-hugging bodice and a full skirt trimmed with hundreds of tiny pearls.

Chrisann broke the news to Raymond at a party thrown by Maurice Wiggan in his flamboyant house situated just outside London. Chrisann was introduced to Maurice's fashionable circle. She nodded, shook hands, smiled and said all the right things. She hated parties of this sort but for the first time her smiles were genuine and she knew it was because for the first time in her life she was really happy. Raymond sauntered up, glass in hand, his dark eyes sweeping over her with approval.

"You look lovely tonight, Chrisann. Glad you've come to your senses about that business with the MacBeth chap. Knew you would in the end."

Chrisann broke her news and Raymond's mouth fell open. "Oh, no," he groaned. "You can't, Chrisann, you simply can't throw all this away, bury yourself in the country—"

"Don't be silly, Raymond, I'm not going to be buried. Believe it or not it's easier to breathe outside of towns." She laid her hand on his arm. "I'm sorry, Raymond, you are sweet and kind in your own way. You know what you felt for me was just a fad, you'll get over it."

He pulled his arm away. "Don't patronize me, Chrisann. I do love you and I won't get over it. How could you do this to me? I would have given you the world, darling, given you sun and blue skies. It rains all the time in Scotland, you'll simply hate it."

"I don't want the world, Raymond," she told him firmly. "I want Ullin MacBeth. He is my world, all I ever wanted of it. And the sun does shine in Scotland, I've seen it and felt it. It does rain, yes, but it's a soft rain in a soft and beautiful land. Oh, be happy for me, please. I – I want you to be Ullin's best man. I've discussed it with him and he's quite agreeable."

Her violet eyes were huge and glowing in her sparkling face. He stared at her broodingly. "How could you ask that of me, Chrisann? I want to be your groom, not your best man. You really are the most thoughtless woman I've ever known."

He sulked for two days before conceding to her wishes. She threw her arms round him and kissed him. "Lucky, lucky MacBeth," he told her. "He must be quite a man to make you give up everything you've worked for to lead the life of a country recluse. You can't live on love you know, darling, or lobsters either for that matter. Oh, damn, it's like talking to a wall! Keats will go off his head when he hears this. You're the star attraction of his agency."

Raymond was right. Anthony threw up his hands in horror and wailed. "Chrisann, I can't let you do this!" he cried. "It's the worst piece of nonsense you've trotted out so far. What about me! What about—"

"You'll survive, Anthony," she said flatly. "Stop acting. Just think of all those dewy-eyed young innocents queuing up at my back. I'm bowing out while I can do so in a dignified way. How awful to wait till I'm thrown out. After all, I'm not getting any younger, you as much as told me that yourself just recently."

"Don't be so damned smart, Chrisann. You've years left in you yet."

She giggled. "You make me sound like a very good second-hand car."

"Hell and damnation! This is not a matter for frivolity. You say this chap is Scottish – lives on some remote island. How will he keep you may I ask? What does he do for a living?"

For some reason Chrisann wanted to keep Ullin's identity guarded for the time being. Anthony was so pompous, it wouldn't do him the least bit of harm to be kept dangling for a while and she answered carelessly, "He looks after sheep, that sort of thing

– oh, and I expect he fishes for lobster in his spare time."

There and then she almost collapsed with mirth. Anthony had gone a bright red and was throwing his arms about in the utmost abandon. "Get out, get out, Chrisann!" he yelled, "before I either hit the roof or hit you."

At the door she turned and said mischieviously, "I really came in to invite you to the wedding. There will be proper cards of course but—"

"Out! Out! Out!" he screamed and she made a hasty exit as the door received the shower of magazines that had been meant for her.

Her last evenings in London passed in a whirl of farewell parties. Lights glittered, glasses chinked, her girlfriends milled about her, romanticizing about her forthcoming marriage, though her married friends smiled rather gloatingly and told her she would soon lose her model's figure when the babies started to arrive. But on the whole everyone was nice to her, even Anthony who had decided somewhat condescendingly to come to the wedding after all.

"I'll give it a year," he predicted. "If you're wise you won't let anything occur that might ruin your figure. Stay as lovely as you are and I ought to be able to rustle up a good contract for you any time. By the way, I know your present contract only has a few weeks to run but I'm hoping you'll see it out."

"Of course, Anthony," she said soothingly. "I'll come back after the honeymoon, I promise."

Raymond took her hand and led her to a corner to talk to her seriously. "You know, darling, if none of this works out I'll be here waiting," he told her, his gaze on the fullness of her lips. "I can't promise to wait forever mind you but I have no foreseeable plans for the future so you can always count on me."

"But, you've started going out with Lorraine," she pointed out.

"Oh, c'mon, darling," he said, smiling faintly. "A chap has to have someone to take around. It means nothing I assure you – besides – she's just a child, sophisticated-looking, I grant you, but she talks in a most meaningless way. You're gorgeous and talented but you've also got brains – you're interesting to be with – besides, there's a very exciting element about you which I personally always found stimulating, a sort of elusive quality."

"A challenge?" she smiled.

"Yes, oh that too of course, but that's hardly fair, Chrisann. . . ."

"Be honest, Raymond, you never got me into bed and you will always wonder what it would have been like."

"C'mon, darling, must you be so blunt?" His handsome, heavy-jawed face broke into a wry smile. "Never could fool you could I? MacBeth's a lucky blighter. He must be quite something for you to have fallen for him so badly. Just what is his secret I wonder, after all, you hardly know him yet he's turned you on so successfully you're all sort of keyed up – as if you can hardly wait—"

"You've said enough, Raymond."

"Sorry, I always did talk too much."

She got up abruptly and mingled, her thoughts stimulated by Raymond's tactless words. She felt her face growing warm because he had hit so accurately at the truth. She did long to know the delirious joy of finally succumbing to Ullin. His lips and his hands had promised her undreamed of delights and every time she recalled the intimacies they had shared she experienced an ache of erotic longing that made her quiver with anticipation.

She hadn't seen much of him during these last hectic weeks and something niggled constantly at the back of her mind. She was reluctant to think about it but it was always there, a doubt over his actual feelings for her. He had never told her in so many words that he loved her yet whenever he saw her his handsome rugged face became alive and his lips on hers swept away all her secret fears.

Her parents had no doubts that she had made a wise and exciting decision and they were thrilled that she would be living so close to them.

"Grand to think you'll be living so near, sweetheart," her father told her, his dark eyes glowing. "It's wonderful," said her mother. "Mull is just over the water so we'll be able to visit quite often."

"You can stay for holidays too," smiled Chrisann. "Strathullin House is big enough for us all though I'm afraid you might find it a draughty old place."

Her mother laughed. "Dad and I aren't too ancient not to be able to contend with a bit of discomfort. Of course we'll come and stay with you when you're settled – how odd, to talk of you as being settled. I hope you won't miss the limelight too much."

"I've had enough of that," Chrisann replied with conviction. "I'm looking forward to a bit of peace and quiet."

"How did Ullin's daughter take the news?" queried Mr McNeil.

"She's delighted," said Chrisann, recalling Kirsty's reaction when she had asked rather tentatively, "Kirsty, do you mind very much about me intruding into your life?"

"Intruding? You're more than welcome into our family. Dad's very strong and independent but I know he's been lonely since I went to college. It's difficult for me to get home as often as I would like but now that he has you my mind will be easier." She tossed her fair mane back from her face and added fervently, "I can't tell you how glad I am he's out of the clutches of Claire Hamilton. She's furious, of course, though at the moment she's rather taken up with her poor old auntie. Knowing Claire she'll make her fortune yet, or rather, she'll collect somebody else's. But never mind Claire, let's talk about the wedding – do you realize you are about to become my stepmother? I won't be able to think of you as such. You're only about nine years older than me so you'll be more like a sister."

Chrisann was aghast. "A stepmother – I – I must admit I never thought of that," she giggled. "I hope I don't turn out to be very wicked."

Kirsty hugged her and they both shrieked with laughter at the nonsense.

After that Chrisann was so absorbed with preparations for her wedding she had little time for anything else. Wedding gifts arrived almost every day and there was such a vast quantity she had to pack them into boxes and send them by rail to Oban to be collected and stored in her parents' house where she had decided to hold her display.

Anthony handed her a substantial cheque. "To help keep you alive when the lobsters stop biting," he told her dryly.

Raymond gave her a bedding set which included an electric blanket. "It will keep out the chill of those Scottish winter nights," he smirked. "Might come in handy if MacBeth fails in his duties as a bed warmer though from the look of him I shouldn't think that's likely."

"If the going gets too hot I'll send it back to you," she replied tartly, annoyed to feel her face reddening.

She was thankful when she left London behind for Oban and when she was finally alone in her own bedroom she stood for a long time at the window gazing at Mull in the distance. She felt strangely unreal. Soon she would be living on the island as Ullin MacBeth's wife – she would be Mrs MacBeth. She put her fingers to her lips and gazed back into the room where she had dreamed her childish dreams. She remembered that often as a small girl she had gazed from the window towards the sea and the islands wondering what the future held for her. How could she have known then that the window was to be a frame for her future? That the islands were to be her home? That a man called Ullin would one day be her husband? She smiled to herself. She was looking at everything in a very romantic light but how could she help herself when after tonight she would no longer be a separate entity? Soon she would belong to Ullin – body and soul.

Feeling overwhelmed by her thoughts she went over to where her dress hung and ran her fingers over the folds of cream silk. "I'll be a good wife to you, my darling," she whispered into the darkness. "And even though you haven't yet told me you love me I don't need words like that to convince me that you do."

But she did need them. As she got into bed and lay staring into the darkness she knew that she needed them very much and she would never be completely happy till he had spoken them.

She awoke to a morning filled with sunshine and it seemed no time at all till she was at the door of the church leaning on her father's arm, nervous and apprehensive.

"You look beautiful," he told her, his dark eyes sweeping over her face framed in its cloud of night-black hair.

"I feel terrible," she confided as she fidgeted with her headdress, a simple tiara of braided cream and flame-coloured rosebuds.

"Stop it, you're perfect," whispered Kirsty. She was one of the bridesmaids, slender and golden in a long cream gown with tiny puffed sleeves. "If you touch that tiara again it will fall to pieces and you'll go into church looking like something the wind blew in."

Mr McNeil grinned and said thoughtfully, "You know, Chrisann, I'm about to give you away yet I feel as if I'm about to have you back. You've lived away from us for so long you were becoming a stranger. Thanks to Ullin we'll be more like neighbours from now on."

The wedding march struck up and she found herself walking up the aisle – no – floating would be more accurate; her dream was about to become reality. Through a blur she saw the kindly faces of Colin Mor, Jean, Mary, Bob, Jamie staring in childish awe. There were lots of faces she didn't know, islanders who were Ullin's friends. Then came the smiling faces of her own family and friends. Her mother sat beside Uncle Theadore who had arrived from Canada the day before, an extremely handsome man with a marvellous black beard and solemn eyes.

She had the sensation of walking on air, gliding towards someone she had waited for all her life – and suddenly there he was, a magnificent creature who stood tall and straight, his blond head slightly bowed, his shoulders filling his lovat tweed jacket, supremely proud in his MacBeth kilt.

Her heart raced and silently she cried, Ullin, I'm here, at last, I'm here. She felt strange, afraid almost of that tall noble figure rigged in the full splendour of Highland dress. She was back again in the past, behind the counter of her father's shop, on the fringe, an outsider looking into the lives of two people who had seemed intent only on each other – then a pair of blue eyes had rested upon her, unseen forces bonded her to him in timeless moments and all through her future life she had been aware of those fragmentary pictures, had remembered Ullin MacBeth, his power, his magnetism.

And now she was beside him, seeing the slight turn of his head, the blue eyes appraising her slowly, approvingly. His arm brushed against hers and his virile warmth beat into her, flooding her veins. His wide sensual mouth relaxed slightly and the apprehension left her. Her soft red mouth parted into a smile and the ceremony began.

Chapter Eleven

In no time at all it seemed they were moving into the brilliant sunshine of the September day. Ullin's hand was strong and warm in hers. The confetti was raining over them, cameras were flashing, everyone was smiling, even her mother who had shed tears in church. Ullin had been against a big society wedding; even so word had leaked out and photographers and reporters from several newspapers jostled to interview the newlyweds. Ullin took Chrisann firmly by the arm and propelled her into a waiting car. The reception was being held in a nearby hotel. Raymond sauntered up and took Chrisann in his arms. "You can't deny me this time, darling, it's my right as best man."

His kiss would have lingered but she pushed him gently away. "Reserving it all for later?" His smile was somewhat forced. "Your lips are very sweet, Chrisann. I'll say it again, MacBeth's a lucky beggar . . . talking of MacBeth . . ." He spun round and caught Ullin by the shoulder. "I say, old man, you're a bit of a dark horse, eh? Not the reticent country gent you make yourself out to be. Came to me when I saw you got up in that rig out, always thought I'd seen you from somewhere. The tattoo in Edinburgh, wasn't it? I was dining at the North British and saw you with a gorgeous redhead. Ah well, no secrets now, married man and all that – again. I had a word with the newspaper chaps and it seems you're one of the landed gentry. I must say, Chrisann pulled the wool over our eyes; must go and tell Keats, I saw him a few minutes ago talking to that redhead I mentioned just now."

Chrisann, already smarting from Raymond's tactless remarks about Ullin and Claire, found panic gripping her at his last words. She had imagined that never again would she have to be in the same room as the mistress of Stonehurst, now, according to Raymond she was actually here. Surely she wouldn't have the nerve to gatecrash the reception. But she was here all right. In a daze Chrisann saw her gliding across the room, the picture of poise in a green velvet dress that showed to perfection her magnificent golden shoulders and the slender column of her neck. Chrisann noticed that Ullin had gone slightly pale but neither of them had time to remark on the situation because Claire was bearing down on Ullin, her amber eyes flashing as she reached him and unhesitatingly wound her arms about his neck to kiss him full on the lips.

"I just had to come and wish you luck," she drawled coolly. "You don't mind, do you, darling? After all you belong to someone else now and I won't get many opportunities like this."

Chrisann felt engulfed by a fear she could put no name to and she was thankful that Jean bustled up just then to hug her and kiss her warmly on the cheek. "Congratulations, my lassie," she beamed. "Ach, but it was the nicest wedding ever – nearly as fine as my own. Colin and myself were married in a wee kirk on Mull and our reception was more of a ceilidh in the village hall but to us it was a very grand occasion. You'll make Ullin happy, I just know it. Since I first saw the pair of you together I knew you were meant for each other."

"Ay, and don't let that Claire spoil things for you,"

put in Mary. "Fancy the cheek of her showing up and her not even invited." She squeezed Chrisann's hand. "I told you your wedding would be the best though I wonder why you didn't have the reception at Strathullin House."

"Ullin said something about the decorators being in." Chrisann's answer was mechanical though all her senses were as taut as bowstrings. Claire's strange amber eyes were upon her and though they were glittering with malice she decided to switch on her charm as she came over to kiss Chrisann on the cheek. "Don't you look lovely, my dear?" she said in silken tones. "But then . . ." she lowered her voice to a menacing hiss, "you've made quite a conquest, haven't you? Hasn't it ever occurred to you Ullin might regard you as the conquest? You'll give him what he wants – and a lot more besides – he knows what he wants and will go all out to get it."

"Just what do you mean by that?" demanded Chrisann, keeping her voice even.

Claire's laugh tinkled out. "Money, my dear," she said in a low voice. "All his little ventures have put him out of pocket and though they will eventually pay off it will take some time. You are successful and rich, that was what swayed him, the only reason he married you instead of me. If the boot had been on the other foot it would be my finger Ullin's rings would be decorating, believe me."

From somewhere Chrisann found the strength to say sarcastically, "Why should I? You tried to chase me away once before with your deceitful lies."

Claire's elegant eyebrows rose. "Did I? Really, Chrisann, you're very naïve, you misconstrued remarks I made in all innocence." A secretive smile lifted the corners of her perfect though petulant mouth. "If I were you I'd keep a close watch on your new husband. Whatever he may have told you you can take it from me we're still very close friends." She paused and with a maddeningly assured laugh added, "You saw for yourself the effect I still have on him. He went quite pale when he saw me just now and it wasn't with anger because he didn't exactly spurn my advances." With a lanquid flick of her wrist she glanced at her watch. "I'm sorry I can't stay to enjoy the fun but I really must be going. Auntie is ill and needs me very much just now. I won't tell you to enjoy your honeymoon – it's a foregone conclusion; Ullin is an expert lover – I can vouch for it." With her chestnut head held high she made a queenly departure which was briefly delayed by two newspaper reporters at the door.

In an attempt to hide her seething feelings, Chrisann lifted a glass of champagne to her lips, hoping that her flaming face would be attributed to the effects of the sparkling drink. From the corner of her eye she watched Claire talking animatedly to the reporters but it was a short interview and as soon as she had disappeared from sight Chrisann took a deep breath and went to seek out Ullin.

"Why didn't you tell her to go away?" she appealed, trying to keep her voice steady. "She had no right to be here."

"Oh, for heaven's sake, Chrisann," he returned somewhat snappishly. "She didn't do any harm and I wasn't going to create a scene over such a triviality."

"What makes you so certain she did no harm?" said Chrisann her face pale with hurt.

"Don't go making mountains out of molehills," he said cuttingly. "I married you, didn't I? You can forget Claire now."

"Can I?" she said bleakly. "The point is – can you?"

"That's enough," he clipped coldly. "This is our wedding day and I won't have it ruined by silly arguments." His gaze travelled over her and she saw naked desire in his eyes. His voice was softer as he added, "Darling, you're mine now and I want only to make you happy. You're so very very lovely, I want to hold you in my arms and never let go. But first, will you dance with me – Mrs MacBeth."

He swept her away and as she danced close to him some of her fears left her. Through the flimsy material of her dress she could feel his heart beating and as he put his lips against her neck her legs trembled as all the familiar responses to him swept through her.

"I can't go on like this any longer," he said into her ear and his voice was husky. "You're so soft, so beautiful. . . ."

The reception was in full swing when they slipped away. He had asked her weeks ago where she wanted to go for the honeymoon and her answer had been prompt. "Ronnach – if you don't mind that is. It all began there and I want to go back to the beginning and savour each moment of our being together." She had laughed and added, "You won't leave me at Ronnach Ferry, will you? Or make me do acrobatics on greasy steps."

"Not unless you go berserk with rage over something trivial," he had replied with a smile.

He was silent as they sat in her Mini Metro on the ferry over to Mull. Raymond had driven the car from London to Oban and she was grateful to him, knowing how much she would need a car of her own on the island. Ullin's tall figure seemed to fill the little car and on arrival at Craignure he got out and stretched and again she was reminded of a tiger lazily stirring from its rest. They left the Metro at Craignure to be collected at a later date and transferred their things into Ullin's Rover which he had left parked near the pier.

He looked right in the bigger car, his long legs had room to work the pedals comfortably. He was still disinclined to speak and she sat beside him, watching the miles slip away, her body growing tense with the sensing of tension in him. She glanced furtively at his handsome profile. It was unsmiling, rather stern in fact, the firm, sensual mouth that had kissed her till she was dizzy with delight, was set into rigid lines. She looked at his hands on the wheel; the hairs were golden in the fading sun. He had taken off his jacket. The sleeves of his white shirt were rolled to the elbows, the muscles of his lower arms stood out, his powerful chest strained against the fine material of his shirt.

She felt very small beside him and she shivered a little as she wondered why he was so silent. He hadn't touched her since dancing with her at the reception. A tiny pang of apprehension trembled through her. They would be alone on Ronnach tonight. Jean and her family were staying the night with relatives in Oban; only Sam the shepherd was coming back to see to the dogs but his cottage was quite a way over the hill from Dykehill and he was such a shy man he kept very much to himself.

Despite herself her thoughts strayed to Claire. Was she the reason for his silence? Was he wishing that she was beside him now? That circumstances had made it possible for him to get Claire *and* Stonehurst. Perhaps, as Claire had suggested with such malice he had run out of money and had only married into it to further his ambitions. . . .

No! Chrisann pushed the thoughts away. She wouldn't let Claire spoil things for her. She had run away once before because of Claire and her bitchiness, she wouldn't allow it ever again to come between her and Ullin. But something *was* wrong. But what? With her? With him? She was married to him now, his rings were on her finger, they were at the start of their honeymoon and she was his bride. Yet – come to think of it – he hadn't said very much at all since leaving the church. . . . How long had she known him? Eight weeks, that was all. He was a stranger to her. She was sitting in a car beside a complete and utter stranger speeding towards a remote Hebridean island. Panic welled in her breast. Nervously she played with her engagement ring, thinking about the time he had given it to her, tenderly and with pride.

The faint aroma of his aftershave wafted to her, emphasizing his manliness, his nearness. Tonight she would lie in his arms and she would surrender her body to him. . . . Her heart fluttered like the fast beating wings of an imprisoned bird. She would fail him. She couldn't go through with it. . . . Suddenly his hand came over to squeeze hers tightly though still he didn't speak.

"Oh, Ullin," she whispered. "I've been sitting here not knowing what to say. . . ."

"Hush," he murmured, "we're nearly there."

The car reached the top of a hill and Chrisann drew in her breath in wonder. The sun was sinking beyond Ronnach and the Treshnish Isles. The beauty of the scene was unbelievable. The red ball in the heavens was suspended above the horizon, the sea rippled to the coastline like a sheet of molten fire. In the bays the water was so calm it mirrored the boats lying at anchor; sheep and cows grazed peacefully on the lush links by the shore; the feeling of languorous tranquillity encompassed everything. Chrisann felt it soaking into her, soothing her. Ronnach lay like a purple jewel on a bed of gold. It seemed to be beckoning to her. It wasn't a dream, it was real, the island where she and Ullin would spend their first days as man and wife.

The journey over to Ronnach was so very different from that first time. Then it had rained, she had been cold, angry and resentful. Now the boat was a cradle, the sea a lullaby, crooning a song of love. She watched the droplets of water showering off the oars like topaz crystals. Ullin was like a bronze statue etched against the sky. He pulled at the oars, steadily, rhythmically. She watched him breathlessly; he watched her, hardly blinking, his mouth unsmiling. She could feel the tension mounting between them, emphasized by the absence of human voice, deepened by the plaintive cries of resting gulls, the lone call of a heron gliding low over the water.

This time he didn't ground the boat on the shore, he tied it up at the jetty and helped her climb the steps. The air was sharp, laden with the keen clean smell of the sea. He slid his arm inside her coat and pulled her in close to him and as they walked she felt the heat of him burning into her till it seemed that his very blood was coursing through her veins. He laid his fair head against her dark one and nuzzled first her hair then her ear. Tingles of pleasure shivered to the very base of her spine. His other arm came round to enclose her even nearer to him and they walked as one, without words, towards the grey stone house set against the dark bulk of the hill.

Chrisann felt as if she was walking through a strange dimension of time. Was it not just yesterday that she had sought shelter from the storm? Pounded on this sturdy door? Found refuge in the safe harbour of the house of Ullin Duncan MacBeth? She was Mrs MacBeth now. The realization came home fully to her. She had sailed through the calm and the storm, the wave and the wind till finally she had found safe anchorage. She smiled a little to herself. She was being poetical again but she couldn't help it. She was encompassed with the sheer solemnity and beauty of these wonderful first hours as the wife of Ullin MacBeth.

At the door he swept her up in his arms and carried her inside. Still holding her he gazed down at the soft full curve of her mouth but didn't kiss her. All the time she felt her limbs growing more and more shaky; she experienced great difficulty in stopping herself from visibly trembling. Mirk barked from the shed and Ullin said, "I'll go and let him out. Make yourself at home, it's yours now."

"Could I have a bath? It – it might help me to – relax." Her voice sounded small, strange to her own ears.

"Darling, you're trembling." He took her firmly by the hand and led her into the living-room. "A drink is what you need, loosen you up a bit. What will it be? Remember, you had champagne at the reception so don't ask for anything too strong."

"Brandy," she said, promptly and recklessly.

His deep laugh boomed. "That night you fell into my arms out of the storm you told me you didn't drink."

"I don't – normally; only when I'm – I'm cold," she said quickly.

He poured two measures of brandy and downed his quickly before he bounded upstairs to run her bath. She heard him coming back down and outside to see to Mirk. Slowly she put her empty glass on the sideboard and putting the tips of her fingers to her lips she gazed all round the cosy room.

"You're here, Chrisann," she breathed and gave a soft little chuckle of delight. Minutes later she lay in the bath, savouring the warmth, going over in her mind every moment of her wedding day. The sun had shone, everyone had been so nice – except for Claire. The thought drummed in her head but she pushed it quickly away.

Even Anthony had forgotten his grievances and had entered into the spirit of the occasion though he had caught hold of her to say, "Don't forget, Chrisann, you know where to come if none of this works out. I for one don't think it will last. Oh, I know you fooled us into thinking your life would revolve round sheep and lobsters. MacBeth's a big landowner from all accounts but most of your time will be spent in the country – God help you! It's no way for a girl like you to live. You'll get bored, mark my words."

"I won't get bored, Anthony," she told him firmly. "I've had all the boring times. At last I've found what I've been looking for all these years – and it's not just a passing whim. This is one contract that won't run out. I'll be back to finish my contract with you; meanwhile I'll send you a postcard – let you know if the lobsters are rising to bait."

She smiled as she remembered his sour smile and the rapid blinking of his eyes behind his thick spectacles. Downstairs Ullin was moving about, talking to Mirk. A door closed and footsteps bounded up the stairs then came along the corridor. She gave a little start and sat up. She had wanted to be ready for him, to be in bed before he came up. The steps didn't stop at the bedroom but came closer and before she could do anything about it he stood in the doorway, filling the space, his eyes full of that amusement she knew so well.

She slid down under the soap bubbles. "Go away, how dare you come in here without knocking, without—"

"For heaven's sake, Chrisann, you're my wife now. If you're so very prudish I'll shut my eyes and not even look at you as I pass. I only came up to have a shower. It's been a long and rather exacting day. Like you I have to unwind."

With eyes fixed straight ahead he went past the bath

and disappeared into the shower cabinet in the corner. Seconds later his clothes were tossed out, one by one till they formed a little mound. The door slid shut and the shower hissed and steamed. Chrisann clapped a soapy hand over her mouth to stifle a giggle. Quickly she rose and stepping out of the bath wound a large towel about her, let the water out of the bath, and dived for the bedroom. It was a fair-sized room, softly lit, the duvet on the large double bed turned down neatly. It was all very tidy, unnaturally so for a place that had been a man's domain and she guessed that Jean had been busy.

Her case was on a chair by the bed. She rummaged through the garments she had packed so carefully the night before. Her hands shook as she lifted the nightdress from its tissue wrappings. It was Grecian style, pure white silk. She and her closest girlfriend Cathy had been shopping in one of London's big stores when she had spotted the gown among a lot of others. He had told her how much he liked the feel of silk and there and then she made the purchase.

"You needn't bother you know," Cathy had said knowingly. "Men never notice what you're wearing, it's what you don't wear that interests them."

Chrisann ran her hands over the cool material and the towel slid down from her body to the floor. Lifting the nightdress up she gazed at it, lost in her thoughts.

"Lovely." The deep voice came softly from the doorway. "The most perfect model for skin I've ever seen."

She jumped and spun round, holding the gown in front of her. Her legs went weak and wobbled beneath her. He was so tall, dressed only in a Paisley silk dressing-gown tied loosely at the waist, his skin glowing from the shower.

"Please, let me put this on," she whispered. "I bought it specially. . . . He shut the door. Without speaking he came towards her. "Ullin, please, you said you liked the feel of silk."

"I like the feel of silken skin better." His voice was hoarse, his eyes intent, devouring her face, her lips – her body. "Don't be afraid, Chrisann, my beautiful darling. I've waited a long time for this moment, so long I thought it was a dream that might never come true. Coming over in the car I was a man in a trance. I couldn't believe that at last you were at my side, that I wasn't going home alone. I didn't know what to say so I said nothing. Now it's just you and me."

He was filling her vision, the look on his handsome face one of deep desire. His blond hair was ruffled and damp, his lips slightly parted to show strong even teeth. He touched her hair, her face. She closed her eyes. His arms came round her, then his mouth came down on hers, firm, warm, tender. She felt herself being lifted up and carried over to the bed. The sheets were cold against her naked back but he had slipped out of his dressing-gown and she felt the heat of him as he lay down beside her. In the soft light his body was golden and so magnificently masculine she experienced a crazy and all-consuming urge to touch him all over. With a helpless moan of resignation she tangled her fingers into the sun-bleached hair at the nape of his neck. His blue gaze was upon her, hungrily devouring the beauty of her slender body then his kisses were on her ears, her neck; slowly his hands started to explore, sliding over her body lightly yet leaving trails of such exquisite warmth she parted her lips and gave a little cry.

"It's all right, it's all right." His voice was faraway. "Relax, relax, my beautiful bride."

His kisses became deeper and more demanding and she gave herself up to this man who had, from the beginning, captured her body and soul.

After that they spoke no words, there was no need for them. His mouth was doing things to her that made her forget all else. She felt the world spinning away. They were enclosed in a sphere of their own, removed from reality, taking, giving, without measure of time. As one in a dream she pulled his head down towards her breasts and arched her back to mould her body further against his. She ran her hands over his broad shoulders, delighting in his strength, loving the pliant rippling of his tensile muscles. Beads of perspiration broke on her brow, their moans of pleasure mingled together as warmth shot through them and all was searing, intoxicating sensation.

The tension spewed out of her limbs; she gave herself up to sweet delirium and an ecstasy so wondrous she couldn't keep back the tears that were trembling behind her lids and afterwards when she lay in the warm circle of his arms her love for him was so strong she had to press her lips against his hair to stop herself from saying his name over and over.

He was asleep, his rugged face relaxed into a softness that made him seem like a small boy. His firm sensuous mouth was just a kiss away and ever so gently she traced the line of it with her finger. How she longed to see his lips forming words she ached to hear, yet she knew that she would never ask him if he loved her; she would wait till he told her of his own free will. If he didn't . . . She pushed the thought away and snuggling against him fell into a deep contented sleep.

She woke to a world of sunshine. The curtains had been pulled back to let in the brightness of a glorious autumn day. The sheep were bleating from the fields; a dog barked; hens clucked. She sighed and stretched, feeling relaxed and happy. Lazily she reached out an arm but the space at her side was empty. At that moment the door opened and Ullin came in bearing two cups of tea which he set down on her bedside cabinet.

"To wake you up, lazybones," he said, giving her a look of such sensuous appraisal she was immediately whirled back to the dizzy delights of her first night as his wife. He was dressed in green cords and the brown Shetland wool sweater she had christened with whisky on that fateful stormy night some weeks ago.

She stretched out her arms to him and he said in a low voice, "If I touch you neither of us will see the light of this beautiful day – and I'm supposed to seduce you, you little temptress."

"Who cares about the things we're supposed to do?" she murmured, her fingers curling over the firm flesh of his shoulders as he bent down to claim her mouth.

"I've a feeling the sun will wait for us," he whispered into her ear. "Much more patiently than I can wait – for you."

They were at breakfast in the sunny kitchen when a quick tap came on the door. Chrisann got up to open it and Colin Mor stood there with a bundle of newspapers in his arms, his beguiling smile coming nervously as he said, "I thought you would like to have these. We got them in Oban."

"Come in and have a cup of tea, Colin," called Ullin.

"Thank you very much but I won't be putting you to any bother," said Colin Mor politely. "We have just arrived home and Jean will be wanting a hand with things."

He hurried away and Chrisann came back to the table to spread out the papers. The wedding photographs leapt out at her and with a shout of joy she cried, "They have described you as a Highland laird, a landowner of considerable wealth and standing. Oh, look, darling, the photos are really quite good though if Raymond saw them he would think otherwise."

She pushed the paper across to him and picked up another. At the bottom of the paragraph about the wedding the reporter had written a small piece about Claire to the effect that though there had been a close relationship between herself and Ullin she bore him no grudges for marrying someone else. They were still good friends and, as they were neighbours, she would be seeing a lot of him and his bride.

"Why did she have to intrude?" Chrisann said bitterly, tossing the paper aside angrily.

Ullin picked it up and glanced at it before saying firmly, "She was making a last stand, that's all. She can't quite get over the fact that I married you instead of her and it's her pride she's protecting." His jaw tightened. "I won't allow it to spoil our honeymoon. Come on, we'll leave the dishes till later. We're going to make the most of our fortnight together."

She allowed him to pull her to her feet, her mood of unease evaporating a little at the feel of his protective arm round her shoulders. Hand in hand they ran to the water's edge. His arm slid round her slim waist. "What would you like to do today, Mrs MacBeth? Fish? Paddle? Walk? Sunbathe? Or go out in *Happy Days*?"

"*Happy Days* please. It will bring back memories of how you almost spanked me in Fingal's Cave."

"And how you nearly tore me to pieces – both emotionally and physically."

"Idiot." She clung to him and laughed.

"Happy?" he asked softly.

"Mmm, I never thought such happiness existed."

"No fears left now?"

She hesitated, longing to tell him of her doubts over his real feelings for her but something made her rebel at voicing the things nearest her heart. In time he would tell her he loved her but for the moment she would let the matter rest. She snuggled against him, loving the feel of his hard strong body. "Last night I was – rather apprehensive but you took all that away when you made love to me. You were so gentle – yet so passionate. And to think I thought of you as a beast and a bully."

"Oh, I'm still rather barbaric and can't promise that you'll ever completely tame the animal in me but in time I may settle down and become very boring.

She buried her face into the warm flesh of his neck and said huskily, "You will never be boring – in fact, sometimes I wonder if I can take the excitement of you. When I'm with you I'm all churned up inside and now that I'm going to be living with you on an island I won't be able to run away to get peace."

"You ran away before," he pointed out, a frown darkening his brow.

"Please, don't let's talk about that. It was the most dreadful time in my life. I was so mixed up, hating you – yet wanting you. I never dreamed for one moment you would come after me and ask me to marry you."

"Didn't you?" he teased.

"Well – perhaps I hoped I would see you again."

He nuzzled her ear with his lips and she shivered with pleasure. "As if I would have allowed you to escape so easily," he murmured, a note of arrogance in his tones as he added, "when I want something – or somebody – I usually get it, or them."

"Yes," she agreed faintly. "Master of all you survey – well I'm one of the MacBeths now and masterful as you may be, you'll find that I have a say in what goes on around here. . . ." She glanced up at him. "By the way, I suppose I ought to go over to Strathullin House and supervise the decorators. I'd like to have a go at making the place as cheery looking as possible."

"Don't worry your beautiful head about that," he said briskly. "Kirsty's so good at these things I left most of the decisions to her. You were so busy down in London and I had a lot to see to here so there didn't seem much point in making a fuss. It's only a quick face lift anyway – if you don't like it we can always change it later."

A thread of annoyance went through her. He could at least have consulted her on the matter but then, she reasoned, she had never spoken to him very much about the ugly old house and it was senseless to start an argument by pressing the point now. She felt no great desire to interrupt the honeymoon just to acquaint herself with a house that didn't particularly appeal to her. She would be mistress of it soon enough, the present was what mattered and she said warmly, "Kirsty has made me so welcome to the family. She's very sweet and we get on so well. Funny – I never dreamt that I would ever be in the role of stepmother – I hope I don't turn out to be a wicked old witch."

He threw back his blond head and laughed deeply then he lifted her high in the air and danced with her. "You silly, wonderful girl, I'm so glad you're mine." The sky and the sea merged as he swung her round and in those carefree moments she felt that all the beauty in the world belonged to them alone.

The honeymoon passed all too quickly. They spent many hours on board *Happy Days* and Chrisann, lulled into a deep state of happiness, wished that such times would never end. But one day, looking through the binoculars to Mull, she spotted Claire riding along the wide white sands, and on several occasions after that she saw the horse and its rider on the Mull shores. For some reason she felt uneasy, and the notion seized her that

Claire had set out deliberately to haunt her but angrily she shook the idea away. It was ridiculous to regard her as a threat. Claire had lost what she had gained. She couldn't do any harm now.

She forgot Claire the day Ullin took her to Lunga. It was a clear bright day and they sat side by side on the grassy plateau and through the binoculars picked out the misted hills of the Outer Hebrides. The inner isles were sharp and it was possible to see the white houses on Tiree and Coll and the great ragged peaks of the Cuillin on Skye.

They gathered armfuls of driftwood and made tea on a smoky fire and ate cold chicken, ham, and tinned fruit. Afterwards she lay in his arms listening enthralled as he told her the history of the Treshnish Isles. She found it strangely exciting when he told her that the isles had once been inhabited; that there was a royal castle on Cairn, a Burgh More; that parts of the Iona Library were believed to have been buried there for safety during the Reformation. She began to see how deep his love of these lands went and could understand. She was already captivated by them though she had known them only briefly.

At the Harp Rock she was overawed by the great precipitous cliffs which were packed with colonies of seabirds. The mass of rock was separated from Lunga by a V-shaped chasm where the sea swirled restlessly over the reefs. She looked at Ullin standing on the rocks, the wind buffeting his powerful frame and whipping his sun-bleached hair. He was at home in such a setting, a man of the wind and the waves, the earth and the rain. Sometimes he was so passionate in his lovemaking she was overwhelmed by his sheer animal virility, yet, on the evening he played the violin to her and she watched, fascinated, as his long fingers extracted haunting tunes, she knew that he also had in him a great love for the aesthetic things in life.

"You appreciate the beauty of the arts," she observed during a break in the playing. He appraised her curvaceous body with lazy insolence, his eyes turning to blue fire as they came to rest on the swell of her breasts. "I appreciate all forms of beauty, especially the female form."

She flushed, a wonder in her that he could so easily make her burn with longing just by looking at her. "Ullin, stop it," she said in a low voice. "I'm being serious. That evening you almost ran me over with your Land Rover I noticed your hands and though, at the time, I thought you might be a farmer, I also wondered if you were an artist or a musician."

His eyes held hers as he caressed the bow. "I am a farmer. This morning I had a phone call and tomorrow I have to go over to Mull on business."

"But – it's the last day of our honeymoon," she objected.

"I'll be back in time for tea. Meantime – hadn't we better make the most of our time here?" His voice was low, laden with intimacy. "Come over here, please, your master has some very pressing business to attend to – now." Mesmerized she obeyed and he pulled her down onto his knee, his exploring hands expertly dispensing with the fastening of her bra while his lips laid a trail of fire from her neck to the soft flesh of her breasts. With a helpless moan of resignation she gave herself up to rapture, forgetting tomorrow, forgetting everything – but him.

He left early the next morning taking the small motor launch he had had brought over from its anchorage in the bay below Strathullin House so that they could play in it during the honeymoon. Jamie, now a proud schoolboy of several weeks, eagerly accepted a ride over to the opposite shore.

"I'll collect him when school finishes," Ullin told Colin Mor. "It will save you a journey."

"How will you manage in the winter?" Chrisann asked Colin as they walked up the shore to the road.

"Ach, I'll manage," said Colin off-handedly. "It's sheltered in this part of the loch but if it plays up rough I'm sure Jamie won't be minding the odd day off school." He chuckled. "When I was a lad I was always plunking lessons. I much preferred working on the croft than struggling to learn sums, though Jamie's a bright lad and I wouldn't like him to miss too much learning. By the way, Bob brought your wee car over from Craignure a day or two back. It's a bit late to be telling you but . . ." He turned his shy gaze on her. "None of us liked to disturb you and if you'd been wanting to go anywhere you would have gone in Ullin's car. Anyway, yours is over at Ronnach Ferry if you should be wanting it though Jean says you are to come along to us if you are feeling like company."

"Thanks, I will," she said warmly and went on over the winding road to Dykehill, vaguely toying with the idea of taking the car and going into Tobermory. She needed several things for the journey to London but they weren't particularly important items and she decided instead to give Dykehill a good cleaning.

The thought of the honeymoon being almost over saddened her a good deal and she was further depressed when she let herself into the house. Despite Mirk and the cats the rooms were strangely empty without Ullin's powerful presence. She felt oddly bereft, as if he had deliberately deserted her for something more important. She was plumping the cushions on the sofa when the phone shrilled from the hall, making her jump.

Claire's honeyed tones came over the line. "Hallo, Chrisann," she drawled, "I was wondering if Ullin has left yet."

"Why yes, he went over about twenty minutes ago," Chrisann volunteered then immediately wished she had been more evasive. She wondered how Claire had found out about Ullin's plans and what her reasons were for checking up on him but before she could say anything Claire said a hurried goodbye and hung up.

Chrisann took a deep shuddering breath and tried not to think of the things Claire had said at the reception. But it was no use. Like poisoned threads the words crept into her mind and it was as if Claire was standing beside her saying warningly, "If I were you I'd keep a close watch on your new husband."

No, no, I won't let her do this! The protest screamed inside her head. For a few moments she fought a fierce inner battle with herself but it was no use. Grabbing her jacket and her bag she ran to the jetty and managed to engage the attention of an old man who was fishing a little way off. Two pound notes persuaded him that it was worthwhile leaving what he was doing to take her over to Ronnach Ferry where she jumped quickly into her car and set off. Her heart beat fast as she passed the gates of Strathullin House and drove on towards the moor road that would take her to Tobermory.

All the time she told herself that her journey was innocent, she only intended to go shopping; she wasn't prying, she wasn't! But all the time she was on the lookout for Ullin's car, guilt tearing her in two. The vast stretches of moor rolled away on either side, the narrow ribbon of road was deserted. When she reached the entrance to Stonehurst she accelerated so violently she almost veered into a ditch and she drove on, her heart in her mouth, towards Tobermory, where she made a few purchases, hurriedly drank a cup of coffee, then got back into her car again.

She half thought of going to see Claire's Aunt Rose. Kirsty had told her the name of the house and it would be an easy enough matter to find out where it was. If Claire was there everything would be all right. But the idea faded quickly. What a fool she would look going to visit an old lady who had never set eyes on her before. She started up the car and left Tobermory behind, all the while wishing that she had asked Ullin where he was going that day and what he would be doing. The term 'business' was vague and, in Ullin's case embraced so many facets of his life. It could be to do with land, livestock, some deal that had to be tied up, in which case he might even be over in Oban. She knew that a man called Donald McDonald managed the Strathullin Estate and that he lived in a house outside Dervaig.

She was nearing that village now and deliberately she made a detour past Donald's house. There was no sign of Ullin's car and with a red face she drove on, her hands shaking on the wheel as it came to her like a hammer blow, just exactly what she was doing. She was spying on Ullin – because Claire had told her to she was obeying like some feeble-minded soul who didn't know any better. Angrily she pulled herself together. She would stop this nonsense. She would go back to Ronnach this minute and make Dykehill warm and welcoming for his return. It was the last evening of their honeymoon and she would make it wonderful. . . .

In the distance she saw Ullin's Rover turning in at the gates of Stonehurst. Her heart seemed to stop beating entirely before it went racing on, thundering against her ribcage with such force she felt the breath squeezing from her lungs. Bringing the Metro to a halt in a nearby passing place she got out and on trembling legs walked to the gates of Stonehurst where she paused for a long breathless moment. Then, straightening her shoulders resolutely she went on, skirting the shrublined drive like a furtive intruder. And that was just what she felt when she finally came to the end of the magnificent driveway and saw Claire and Ullin walking close together on the beautifully kept terrace in front of the house.

Claire's voice floated clearly. "Darling, this is just like old times! I've missed you more than I can say. What excuse did you make to your new little wife?"

"That I had business to attend to." Ullin's deep voice reverberated against Chrisann's ears like a thunderclap.

Claire laughed delightedly and cried, "Would you like to know what business I have in mind!" With a sudden swift movement she twined her arms round Ullin's neck and pulled his head down.

Chrisann could bear no more. With a strangled sob she turned and ran back to the car, feeling her world collapsing like a flimsy matchbox tower. He had deceived her! He had married her but he still wanted Claire! Her throat constricted so tightly she could barely swallow and as she started up the car and drove away she could hardly see the road ahead for tears. The hurt and anger she had thought buried forever came rushing in on her and completely engulfed all her powers of reasoning.

By the time she reached Ronnach Ferry pride had taken the place of anger and on the journey over to Ronnach she vowed that she wouldn't say a word to him about what she had seen. If his visit to Claire had been innocent he would mention it and everything would be all right. It had to be, she told herself miserably, as she handed Dave some money for bringing her over.

Chapter Twelve

She reached Dykehill to find the fire leaping warmly in the grate and Jean bustling in the kitchen.

"Jean," she said dazedly. "What on earth are you doing?"

"Preparing a nice meal for the last evening of your honeymoon, nothing special mind but it will save you doing it and give you more time to be with Ullin." She glanced at the carrier bags in Chrisann's hands. "I see you've been shopping. I thought you would have been longer. When I go to Tobermory I'm usually away for the day."

"It was quiet," said Chrisann quickly, sinking down on a chair by the table. As if by magic the teapot was placed in front of her and Jean brought out two cups. Soon they were sipping tea and chatting companionably.

"What a pity you have to go back to London tomorrow," sighed Jean. "It's been a pleasure having you about. I miss Mary and though she's just over the water I don't see her as often as I would like."

Impulsively Chrisann put her hand over Jean's and said warmly, "Oh, Jean, you've no idea how I've loved being here. I feel so at home in this house. I'm going to miss you terribly. I wish you could come over to Strathullin House and keep me company."

Jean shook her head. "It would be fine if I could. To tell the truth Colin and myself are not as young as we were and now that Jamie is at school it isn't so easy. Colin won't admit it but I know fine he isn't looking forward to taking the boat over in the winter." She shrugged her shoulders and smiled. "Ach, we'll manage, and what would you be wanting me for when you have Ullin to keep you company. You'll have a busy life as mistress of Strathullin. You'll be no sooner back from London than you will be whisked away to Inverness. Ullin works very very hard when he's here but he relaxes with the fishing when he goes up to Inverness."

Chrisann bent her head to hide the flush on her face. How rosy Jean made the future sound – if only things were that simple – if only today could be wiped out she could be happy again and look forward instead of back. She dreaded seeing Ullin again and to get her mind away from everything she began to talk quickly – and asked Jean a question that immediately brought back all her fears and doubts. "How is Claire's auntie?" she said and could have bitten out her tongue because she didn't want to talk about anything connected with Claire.

"As well as she'll ever be, she's a tough old woman and could hang on for years yet."

"But – according to Claire she's been dancing attendance on her aunt because she's ill. The way Claire spoke the old lady seemed about to die."

Jean snorted. "Wishful thinking more like. She's dying to get her hands on Rose's money. As for dancing attendance, our Claire Hamilton is the one who likes to get all the attention – ay – and she'll get it too the way she flaunts herself. Mark my words, she'll get by financially; she'll have some man dangling on the end of a string, always did."

There and then Chrisann almost fainted but somehow she hung on though with every passing minute the feeling of trepidation grew inside her so that by the time she finally heard Ullin's firm tread in the hall her nerves were curled into a tight knot in her stomach. He didn't come straight into the living-room but went first into the kitchen where she heard him talking to Jean. Their voices became more hushed and in a state of near panic Chrisann looked around the room like a haunted animal seeking an escape. Jean had set the table beautifully, even going to the trouble of placing candles into wine bottles to give the meal a romantic touch. It was such a typically thoughtful gesture Chrisann bit her lip and felt like crying. Instead she went to the door and opening it quietly flew upstairs to run a comb through her hair and add a touch of rouge to her pale cheeks.

She came down to find Jean gone and Ullin sitting by the living-room fire sipping at a glass of whisky. "Would you like one?" he asked and she nodded, her hands like ice though the room was warm. Slowly he uncurled his lithe frame from the chair and padded over to the sideboard. When he handed her the glass she took it too quickly, spilling some onto the rug.

"What's the matter, you're shaking." He stood in front of her, his tall powerful body blotting out the lamplight, his blue eyes boring into her questioningly.

"I'm – I'm a bit cold, the bedroom is a bit chilly." She was annoyed that her voice was as shaky as her hands.

"Jean tells me you went into Tobermory today." He sounded suspicious, his tones were curt and rather cold.

She nodded and said too brightly, "That's right, I had to get some things to take with me tomorrow. What – what did you do?"

She made the question sound like a careless afterthought and just as carelessly he answered. "I told you – business – nothing you need bother your head about."

She laid her drink down. "I think we'll have the meal now – I'm a bit tired and would like to have an early night so that I can get an early start in the morning."

Her voice was low and muffled and turning she hurried into the kitchen where she placed her hands on the table to steady herself. She took a long shuddering breath. He hadn't said a word about visiting Claire; he had deliberately evaded her question. He was deceiving her and he had been distant – so much so he was like a stranger she didn't know at all.

Somehow she got through the evening though all she wanted was to creep up to bed and be alone, yet, he was so aloof and silent during dinner, she might well have been sitting at the table by herself. The meal was simple but delicious, cold lobster salad washed down with a mild white wine, followed by a mouthwatering strawberry flan smothered in fresh cream. Chrisann toyed with her food and covertly looked at Ullin sitting opposite. His rugged face was honed to bronzed smoothness in the light from the candles. He had his back to the fire and every pliant muscle in his strong body was etched against the orange glow; his hair was a sheaf of pale gold; his eyes dark pools that glinted mysteriously. Broodingly he ate his food but didn't quite clear the plates she set before him.

When finally he spoke she jumped with fright and dropped her spoon. "Shall we go for a walk?" he asked, frowning a little as he caught sight of her untouched dessert.

"All right," she acceded, "I'll get my jacket."

With Mirk at their heels they walked over the springy turf to the little sandy bay where she had camped. The sea was calm, the Treshnish Isles were blue and appeared to be floating on the hazed horizon. Oyster catchers whistled among the rocks; curlews bubbled out their wondrous song. It was idyllic, so serene and lovely Chrisann felt the tears springing up to her eyes. The sigh of the ocean whispered into the bay and washed over her senses. She belonged here! She belonged! Her heart cried out in sweet affirmation even while her spirit drowned in pain and hurt.

Ullin's arm came out to grasp her slender waist tightly. He felt strong and exciting but rather tense. She stole a glance at him. His handsome profile was rigid, his wide firm mouth unsmiling. She wondered what he was thinking.

"Why are you trembling, Chrisann?" he demanded suddenly.

"I'm – I'm not."

"Yes you are, you've been keeping your distance ever since I got back."

"I haven't – what about you?" she faltered.

"Never mind me. Stop damned well pretending and tell me what's wrong."

"Nothing's wrong – I'm – I'm just tired. You're imagining things."

"No – you are." With a thumb and forefinger he gripped her chin and forced her head round so that her face was just inches from his. "Listen to me," he ordered tersely. "I want you to postpone your trip to London for a day or two."

"Why on earth should I?" she gasped.

"Because I say so."

"Who are you to tell me what to do?"

"In case you've forgotten – I'm your husband."

"Really," she said faintly.

"Yes – really. Phone Anthony tomorrow and tell him you have been unavoidably detained."

"And just who's going to make me?" she cried angrily.

"I am – by force if necessary. There's something that's got to be settled before we go any further – something very important." His voice had grown persuasive, tinged with the tenderness that never failed to tumble her defences.

"All right," she agreed even while she hated herself for her own weakness. She made to move away but he reached out and pulled her into the steely grip of his arms. She tried to struggle away but as his lips claimed hers possessively she ceased to fight him. With a low moan that was near to despair she melted against him and responded to him wildly even while she loathed herself for being so weak that she would allow him anything he asked of her.

Abruptly he released her and she felt as if she had just been slapped on the face. "Let's get back," he said decisively and as he put his arm about her shoulders and they walked home she wondered desperately what it was that had to be settled but knew there was no point in pursuing the matter.

He was in a very enigmatic mood and that night she lay beside him, awake long after he had fallen asleep, staring at the ceiling, feeling uneasy, a million questions filling her head. She turned to look at him. The new moon was rising over the sea and everything in the room was quite visible. His head was snuggled against her shoulder. His hair was rumpled and flaxen bright in the moon's pale beams. The powerful muscles of his bare shoulders and back were relaxed, one brown arm was round her waist, strong and protective – yet – she was feeling far too unsettled to be comforted by physical embraces. If only he could protect her from the harsh evidence of treachery she had witnessed that afternoon.

She knew he suspected she had seen something he hadn't wanted her to see and the fact that he hadn't brought his suspicions into the open only made things worse than they already were. Restlessly she wriggled out of his grasp and went to the window to stare out at the beauty of the silver-bathed sea in the distance. It was so hauntingly lovely she wanted to reach out and embrace the purity of it to her heart.

"Chrisann, what is it?" His voice came sleepily.

"I – don't know."

"Come back to bed, you'll catch cold."

She slipped back into bed and he enclosed her once more in his arms. "Ullin?"

"Yes."

"Why don't you want me to go away tomorrow?"

"Wait and see."

"No!" she protested angrily. "I can't sleep for thinking about it. Tell me now."

His fingers dug deeply into the soft flesh of her arm and he gritted, "Go back to sleep, Chrisann."

"Let go of me, you're hurting; sometimes I – I hate you, Ullin," she finished with a gasp as his fingers bit deeper.

"Do you?" he asked laconically. He pulled her in closer. "Maybe I'd better prove to you that, while there are times you might feel you despise me, at the same time you can't resist me – you never could."

"No." She tried to struggle away. She couldn't allow herself to give in to him because if she did it would only serve to weaken the anger she was building up against him and she needed to be angry; it was the only strength she had when she was in his self-assured presence. She had been almost relieved when he had allowed her to go up to bed before him and when he had finally come in she had pretended to be asleep. He was forcibly pressing the contours of her body against his, and all the while he was nuzzling her ears, searching for her mouth, with a thumb and forefinger clamped round her jaw pulling her head round so that she couldn't turn away again.

His broad chest was pinning her; the steady thumping of his heart reverberated into her.

For a long moment he gazed down at her face in its frame of silken black hair. In the moon's light she could see the desire clouding the blue brilliance of his eyes, tensing his jawline, then hungrily his mouth claimed hers and while his tongue probed the moist warm recesses of her mouth his lithe limbs were stirring. The pulsing heat of his body burned her flesh; without letting her go he raised himself up and moulded himself on top of her. With every shred of willpower she possessed she fought with herself; she kept her limbs rigid; she closed her eyes to shut out the sight of his superb shoulders rippling in the moonbeams spilling across the bed.

One hand brutally and effectively quelled her struggles, the other began to explore her body masterfully, lingering on her breasts. Chrisann drew in her breath, despite herself she felt her limbs relaxing, becoming more and more pliant, more willing to accommodate the eager searching thrusts of his persuasive loins. She gave a little cry as all the familiar responses to him swept through her, dissolving away her anger and leaving only a raw sweet craving for fulfilment. She knew then that it wasn't him she was fighting, it was herself, struggling against her own pitiless instinct to yield to him, no matter what he had done or might do in the future.

She raised her arms to tangle her fingers through his hair and as she heard his breath indrawn with excitement she gave herself up to the rapturous delights he was invoking in her.

Without warning he moved away from her and his voice came mockingly and harshly. "You see, Chrisann, you can't resist me; no matter how hard you try you never will."

His rejection left her feeling as if she had been doused

with icy water. She felt suddenly numb with shame that he had such control over her emotions, she, who until recently had been an independent entity, governing her own life, capable of arranging things to suit herself. Now it seemed he owned her entirely and she simply couldn't bear the idea of that. "You're a despicable beast," she said weakly. "You haven't changed, have you? Still an arrogant brute who thinks it smart to degrade something that ought to be beautiful between a man and a woman."

With a soft little laugh he leaned over and pressed his lips to her hair. "It is beautiful, darling, but I can't have you telling me you hate me just because something doesn't happen to please you. Now, go to sleep like a good girl and the morning will be here before you know it."

He turned away from her and lay down, leaving her wide awake and fuming. She fell into a fitful sleep as dawn was breaking and woke with a start to find the bed empty and the hands of the clock at ten-thirty. With a gasp she rubbed the sleep from her eyes and swinging her legs out of bed donned her blue wool dressing-gown. Running downstairs she found the house to be empty and with a cry of outrage she dashed back upstairs to shower quickly.

When she got back downstairs he was in the kitchen cooking bacon and eggs. He turned from the stove to appraise her admiringly. She wore a green soft wool dress that clung to her curves. A matching hairband held her cloud of dark hair back from her face.

"Lovely," he approved, and there was a gleam of laughter in his eyes.

"Why didn't you wake me?" she shouted, rage getting the better of her.

"You had a harrowing night, darling, I thought you needed to sleep on," he answered carelessly.

"Oh, did you, indeed? I suppose my plans aren't all that important to you, but they are to me. You were the one who asked me to forego my trip to London. . . . You knew I had to phone Anthony to let him know I wouldn't be coming today."

"Temper, temper," he chided patiently. "I had to go out early to help Colin Mor and Sam bring the sheep down from the hill. The cross-breeds are ready for mating."

"Pity the poor sheep!" she yelled furiously. "If the rams perform as poorly as their owner there will be precious few lambs next spring."

"So, that's it," he said with infuriating calm. "Well, if it will make you feel any better we'll leave breakfast till later and go upstairs now to finish off what we started last night."

"What *you* started!" she threw at him, goaded beyond endurance, then, completely losing her control she snapped, "why did you have to go and visit Claire yesterday? I saw you so you needn't deny it!"

His eyes narrowed to steel blue chips and she could gladly have bitten out her tongue, if only to save her pride, but it was too late, there was no going back now.

"So, now we are getting somewhere," he clipped harshly. "I suspected there was something far wrong with you last night."

"You didn't tell me," she cried. "I asked what you had been doing but you evaded the issue. If you had mentioned that you had gone to see her I wouldn't have minded."

His arm shot out and his fingers clamped round her arm as he grated, "Wouldn't you, can you honestly expect me to believe that, can you, Chrisann?"

"Well – perhaps I would have—"

"Of course you would!" he cut in roughly. "Now, I'll explain everything to you later. We are not going to mention Claire's name for the rest of the morning. I've had about all I can take on that score. You are going to phone Anthony then you are coming in here and we are going to eat breakfast like two civilized people."

"You've got a cheek to count yourself civilized—" she began but gasped as his fingers tightened round her arm and she was forced to say, "all right, you win – for the moment. All of this had better have a good explanation because I'm like you – I too have had enough of Claire Hamilton. She's ruined our honeymoon," she ended bitterly.

"Chrisann," he pulled her against him and brushed her lips tenderly with his, "it was a wonderful honeymoon, only the last part was spoiled. Now," he gave her a little push, "go and make your phone call then come back here before my culinary efforts are completely spoiled."

Anthony wasn't too surprised or angry when she spoke to him. "MacBeth must be quite something," he said suggestively. "Go ahead and enjoy yourself, Chrisann, I'll hold off for another couple of days."

She put the phone down and marched into the kitchen to say, "That's that, Anthony has given me his blessings. I hope you're satisfied."

"Delighted, now sit down and eat this and I don't want to see you picking at it."

But she did. It was beautifully cooked and nicely served but she was far too nervous and apprehensive to even finish a slice of toast. Ullin's jaw tightened but he said nothing. Finally he stood up and said tersely, "Right, go and get your jacket. The sooner all this is straightened out the better."

They had just closed the front door behind them when Bob arrived in a rather excited state and addressed himself to Ullin. "We're needing a bit of muscle. Old Fladda has got caught with the tide and is sinking in the sands. We'll need ropes and the tractor to haul her out."

Old Fladda was a cantankerous Highland cow with an insatiable liking for the sea, often going to stand in it for hours at a time. Chrisann had thought it funny the first time she saw the shaggy-coated old beast paddling in the shallows but she didn't think it so funny now.

"I'm sorry, darling." Ullin spread his hands in appeal. "I'll try not to be too long."

"Oh – take all day if you like!" Chrisann threw at him and stormed back into the house.

The afternoon was almost over when he finally put in an appearance and without any sort of explanation for being so long he told her, "Don't bother cooking anything, Jean has invited us to tea; we can't go off hungry."

"I am not hungry," shc told him shortly but she went along with him and managed somchow to get through the meal. It was almost six when they finally took their leave. When they got back to Dykehill he gave her a little push in the direction of the stairs. "Go up and change, it's colder now."

She looked down at the wool dress. "Won't this do? I don't feel like changing."

"Go and change into something warm," he said insistently, his eyes beginning to snap. "Stop being so difficult, you're behaving like a baby."

"You're treating me like one."

"Chrisann, if you don't do as you are told I'll carry you upstairs and undress you myself."

The determination in his blue eyes made her fume. She knew he was perfectly capable of carrying out his threat and she stamped away, almost colliding with him some minutes later when she emerged wearing black cord slacks and a natural coloured Fair Isle sweater.

"That's better," he approved, running his hands intimately over her arms. "Give me a few moments to get out of these trousers. Old Fladda wasn't exactly in raptures when we hauled her out of the sea. She doused us all in mud before she took to her heels."

Some time later he came running downstairs, his fair hair neatly brushed back, his camel slacks and brown sweater smelling of fresh air. He was struggling into a brown cord jacket as he came towards her. "Let's go then, put on your jacket."

She lifted a warm coat from the sofa and threw it round her shoulders but he took it from her and made her push her arms into it. She took a long lingering look round the room. The clock ticked peacefully on the wall, the brassware gleamed warmly in the glow from the fire's embers. Mirk was sitting with his ears pricked in alertness, waiting for the command that would take him to his master's side. Chrisann sighed, longing with every fibre to stay on in the place where she had found such happiness. She felt uneasy about the future and wished it were possible to make time stand still.

Mirk whimpered and Ullin said, "Come on then, boy, it's time to go home."

This is home, Chrisann thought, but she said nothing and stood in the dusk, shivering a little as Ullin closed the door of Dykehill behind him. Silently they walked to the jetty and his strong hands steadied her as they made their way down the steps and into the little motor boat. The roar of the engine was like a profanity tearing the peace apart. Ronnach slipped away. The shades of night were all around it and it looked as if it was slumbering in an endless dream. The lights shone from Colin Mor's house, shimmering down into the water like moonbeams, and even though the house was soon hidden by trees the reflections trembled over the sea till a gust of wind swooped low over the water and left blackness in its wake.

Chapter Thirteen

It was raining by the time they reached Ronnach Ferry; a persistent drizzle that blotted out the hills and the sea. Even so there was colour everywhere: the bracken was golden and the blossoming heather a delicate shade of purple. They passed the lay-by where she had had her first encounter with Ullin. The memory of that evening came back vividly: her enchantment with Ronnach and its green terraced hills; her eagerness to camp there; her boiling indignation when the Land Rover had appeared and spattered her with mud – and later – her conflicting emotions of hatred and desire bred in her by this big virile man who sat so silently by her side, seemingly engrossed in negotiating the car over the narrow winding road.

They passed the Falls of Laggan, a great cascading waterfall pouring down from the hills and, as the road climbed higher, the grey shapes of the Treshnish Isles appeared. They looked distant and remote and it seemed impossible that just recently they had picnicked on Lunga under blue skies. The waters of Loch Tuath were slate-blue, the tops of the waves frisking into white horses in the rising wind. They were approaching the entrance to Strathullin House but the car didn't slow down; instead it accelerated and she cried, "Ullin, where are we going? I want to know – this second."

"You will soon enough," he answered with infuriating calm. "We're nearly there."

"Nearly where?" she demanded but he refused to be drawn and she knew it was useless to pursue the matter though she felt like screaming with frustration.

The road wound through woods of scrub oak and hazel which gave way to lush parkland surrounded by a high wall. "You can relax now, we're here." Ullin's voice was tense. He guided the car through a wide gateway and up a rather rough road flanked by outbuildings. They bumped over a planked bridge where a river rushed in foaming splendour, and came to a sprawling farmhouse with two floors and dormer windows. Roses grew in gay abandon over the weathered grey walls; an assortment of cats were clustered round the doorway; chickens clucked amongst the farm machinery in one of the outhouses.

Ullin guided the car through another set of gates and now the rough road merged into a smooth drive brightly littered with yellow chestnut leaves. "This road goes on to the stables," Ullin said, inclining his head towards a stone archway. "We go in here."

How many gates? wondered Chrisann as they drove through ornamental wrought iron gates which were thrown back. Velvet lawns stretched, merging into acres of green fields. The grey turrets of the Scottish Baronial mansion that was Stonehurst came into view and Chrisann cringed back against her seat. They had come in by a different entrance to the one she had so furtively traversed the day before. The wheels scrunched on the red gravel chips of the driveway, stretching every nerve in her body. The façade of the beautiful house was overwhelming; there seemed to be countless windows, some with balconies where tubs of geraniums made gay splashes of colour.

"Why are you bringing me here, Ullin?" she demanded, her voice low with horror.

Without replying he brought the car to a halt. "This

is Stonehurst," he said, something in his voice she couldn't define.

"I know," she answered tremblingly. "I saw it yesterday; I saw *you* here yesterday – with Claire."

With that lithe grace she knew so well he uncurled himself from his seat and getting out came round to open the door for her, his hand outstretched.

"I'm – I'm not going in there," she said shakily. "I suppose you think this is funny. Well, if it's some sort of joke it's in very poor taste."

"Chrisann, this is no joke." His voice was dangerously level. "I want you to come out of there this minute or I'll haul you out and you won't like that."

"No, I'm not coming," she stated flatly. "You must be mad to think I would ever set foot inside . . ." The words died in her throat as he reached into the car and none too gently assisted her out. His bruising fingers gripped her elbow and he steered her towards the entrance of Stonehurst. Stubbornly she dug her heels into the gravel. "No!" she protested desperately. "I'm not setting foot in that house! Why are you doing this, Ullin?"

"I'll carry you in," he threatened, his voice calm but cold. "And you won't like it, I warn you. There are people inside waiting to meet you."

"What people? What is all this?" she cried but he strode on without answering, his steely grip on her arm forcing her to go with him. He led her through arched wooden doors and a wide porch which opened into a spacious hall where a log fire burned brightly. Several people were in the hall. Chrisann felt her head lightening. Who were they? What was happening to her? Ullin propelled her forward and introduced her. Automatically she responded, shook hands, smiled. She was confronted with a smooth-skinned, pleasant-looking woman.

"This is Mrs Munro." Ullin's voice seemed to come from

a long distance. "She's been housekeeper at Strathullin for as long as I can remember, now she's come here to be with us. She'll be living in one of the cottages near the farm."

Chrisann tried to look suitably impressed. Vaguely she caught some of the other names: Mrs Maitland, the cook; Margery the general help; John Anderson the stud-groom – more, quite a few more but her whirling brain was beyond taking them in. The smile was frozen on her face, her hands felt cold. Everyone murmured something then dispersed. She glanced round in panic, looking for the door. The room spun. Paintings, tapestries, a stag's head whirled and merged together, crushing her, closing her in. She recognized these things, she had seen them at Strathullin House; the fact that they were here could mean only one thing. Ullin had bought Stonehurst.

He had told her it didn't matter if he had to give up the idea of owning Stonehurst but he had lied, it had mattered to him very much – and he expected her to be glad that he had bought a house that had belonged to his former mistress. A house in which he and Claire had shared intimacies – made love. She put her fist to her mouth to stop from crying out in protest, hardly aware that he was leading her through the house, showing her into rooms.

Downstairs there was a study; a library; a tower room, quaint and cosy; kitchens bigger than all the rooms of her Kensington flat put together. The large airy sitting-room smelled of lavender polish; fire shadows danced on an ornate ceiling and gleamed on antique heirlooms. Chairs of padded leather sat on a beautiful Persian carpet; a tiger skin rug sprawled elegantly by the hearth, its yellow eyes glittering, the pride of its spirit captured in the defiance of the snarling jaws.

A flight of broad stairs led to the bedrooms. Chrisann

stumbled along in a daze, saying nothing. Only two rooms made an impression on her mind: one in which a large rocking horse smiled mysteriously, its chipped paint telling of much usage, and another which Ullin told her was the master bedroom. It was blue and gold and smelled of fresh paint. A connecting door led into a dressing-room, another into a gold-carpeted bathroom which contained a shower and a sea-blue suite.

"Kirsty chose the colour scheme but if you don't like it we'll get it changed." Ullin was elated, his voice held notes of triumph. Downstairs once more in the sitting-room he spun her round to face him. "Well, what do you think?"

"Impressive." Her mouth felt frozen. "Impressive and big."

"It will shrink." His eyes glinted with amusement. "There are still some things to be brought from Strathullin. Everything you see here came from there – even the old rocking horse upstairs; generations of MacBeth children have played on it, including myself and my brother. It's been stored away for years but in this house it will come into its own again." His eyes grew very intense. "You see," he continued slowly, "this is where I belong. This house belonged to my family for aeons. It used to be known as Strathullin and will be again because I intend to have its title restored back. Most of the lands round here used to be known as Strathullin till my great-grandfather fell on hard times and had to sell the house and a good portion of the land. Gradually my grandfather built up the family fortunes then it fell to my father. It was his dearest wish to see the house in MacBeth hands once more. It has never had a settled owner since my great-grandfather's day. The Hamiltons have only been here a mere twenty years."

He took her cold hands and led her over to the fire but she didn't sit down, instead she took a few steps back from him, the questions piling into her head so fast she didn't know where to begin.

Before she could say anything he spoke again. "When Claire's father died I thought I stood a chance of buying the place. He wasn't a good businessman and the money he left was swallowed up in death duties. Claire's like her father, she has no business head and doesn't know how to run an estate of this size—"

"But she proved more stubborn than you bargained for," cut in Chrisann. "She wanted to remain the mistress of Stonehurst and one way was to try and get you to marry her—"

"But she didn't succeed," he clipped, his face darkening. "I married you and gave up the idea of owning Stonehurst. Claire was furious when she heard of my intentions but she was desperate by then and couldn't afford to be fussy about where to look for help. She had left things a bit too late and was in quite a state. She had deluded herself into thinking that her Aunt Rose was ill enough to be dying. As it happened the old lady only had a bad dose of flu and made a rapid recovery but to save face Claire gave everyone the impression that she was about to inherit a fortune. All that rubbish she spun the reporters was just to pull the wool over everyone's eyes because she had already approached me and offered to sell the estate. It went against her grain though and she got up to all sorts of mean tricks to make life unpleasant for me. I was furious when she showed up at the wedding. I had asked her not to tell you about this deal as I wanted it to be a surprise and I thought she had come to cause trouble."

"A surprise it certainly is," said Chrisann, still feeling uneasy about the turn of events.

"I bought Stonehurst for you, Chrisann," he said, and there was a hint of steel in his voice. "A sort of wedding present if you like. I know you didn't like the other house; in a way I can understand my first wife disliking it—"

"I would have grown to like it," she cried, "more than I could ever like it here. Claire's in this house, I can feel her all around me – watching."

"Fanciful rubbish," he said sharply.

"Is it? Was yesterday fanciful rubbish? I saw you with her – outside – and you weren't exactly fighting her off."

"I never took Claire seriously," he snorted derisively. "And yesterday was no exception. I had business to discuss with Donald and somehow she found out I'd be at the other house, an easy enough matter in these parts. She phoned me from her aunt's place and asked me to meet her here. She made a great fuss, running to welcome me, clinging round me. It was almost as if she was doing it all for somebody else's benefit because the whole thing turned out to be a farce. She said she only wanted to see me again to wish me well."

Chrisann reddened and she blurted out, "It was for me – my benefit. She – she told me to watch you; she implied that you and she were still – close. She phoned me at Dykehill yesterday and asked if you had left—"

"You didn't fall for that one!" He gave a shout of disbelieving laughter. "Well, well, even I didn't think she could stoop that low. You dear little idiot, you played right into her hands. She was trying to drive the wedge in, Chrisann, she's so jealous of us she can't seem to help herself."

She looked at him. He was standing with his back to the fire, a superbly masculine figure that filled her vision. Somehow he looked right in this house, he belonged, he had got what he wanted – even though it might not be what she wanted.

"What will happen to the other house?" she heard herself ask woodenly.

"I've applied for permission to erect holiday chalets in the grounds and to turn the house into a country club with a swimming pool and sauna. The land isn't good for anything else."

"But these lands are?"

"Yes, 3,000 acres of excellent grazing with another 2,000 acres of rough grazing surrounding the shooting lodge on the other side of the river. It isn't easy being a landowner these days. You have to be ruthless, to decide what is good for farming and what is best done away with. . . . Chrisann," his voice became low and persuasive, "I'm not the sort to sell just for the sake of raking it in. I'd never exploit the countryside that way, I love it too much. In a way I'm keeper of the lands I've inherited and I would never take advantage of my position – you know how much I love these islands, how much I enjoy working close to the earth."

"Yes, Ullin, I know," she said softly, her heart pounding as the tender notes in his voice caressed her ears like music. If only the song was for her, she thought bitterly; if only he spoke of his love for her the way he spoke about the land she might be better able to take everything he had sprung upon her with the complete assurance that she would accept living at Stonehurst without question, sleep in a bed that perhaps he had once slept in with Claire. She couldn't take it and she knew it was because she was jealous of the memories that this house would have for him, memories that she had no part in.

Yet – she loved him so much it was like a flame that consumed her very spirit. How could she turn her back on him? Walk away from him? She would never be able to forget; the biggest part of her would remain with him. She couldn't walk away from that – ever. She wanted to run to him, to be enclosed in his powerful arms, to know the rapture of his lips pressed against hers. . . . His next words slashed across her ears like icy rain.

"Chrisann, I hope you won't mind living quietly for a while. Buying Stonehurst has been a bit of a financial drain – Claire stuck out for as much as she could get." He turned to face her and his eyes were dark pools in his bronzed handsome face. "It doesn't matter, does it, Chrisann? We're partners now and it's a case of share and share alike."

She didn't want to analyse what he meant but Claire had planted the seeds in her mind and she couldn't stop herself. He hadn't bought Stonehurst for her, he had bought it for himself. It had been his burning ambition to own it regardless of the cost. He was a hard-headed businessman and he didn't care who he used to further his ends. If he had told her he loved her things would have been different. She would gladly have given him everything she owned but the only time the word love had crossed his lips had been when he was talking about land. He had told her he needed her, wanted her, as if she was a piece of property that he simply had to get his hands on.

There was a knock on the door and it opened to admit Donald McDonald apologizing for interrupting and going on to say that he had brought the Land Rover down from Strathullin in case Ullin might be needing it.

"Thanks, Donald, that's grand," said Ullin. "You'll stay and have a dram. I'm in the mood for celebrating."

Donald was introduced to Chrisann and she managed to smile and say a few polite words before she excused herself and went out of the room. She had to get out of the house; she had to be alone for a while to think – to decide about her future. In seconds she was outside, her feet crunching on the driveway as she made her way over to the Rover and wrenched the door open. Diving inside she turned the key in the ignition but the engine had grown cold and turned sluggishly. She fumbled for the choke and pulled it out; the engine spluttered into life.

At a reckless pace she drove down the drive and through the gates. It was pitch dark and she felt along the dash panel for the light switch. The sidelights came on but that was all. She had never driven a Rover before and had no earthly idea what all the switches were for. The lack of headlights put her at a disadvantage but it was possible to see the road in front of the bonnet. She bounced around in her seat as the smooth driveway merged into the rough track. The wheels bumped over the bridge and soon the farm buildings and outhouses disappeared from view and she was out on the road.

Unconsciously she steered the car in the direction of Ronnach Ferry. Suddenly she wondered just where she was going. She couldn't go back to Ronnach and she couldn't go back to Stonehurst. The thought struck her that she could drive to Craignure and get the ferry over to Oban where she could stay the night with her parents before travelling on to London. No, no, she thought angrily. How ridiculous that would look. Running home to mummy and daddy at the first hint of a rift in her marriage.

She straightened her shoulders and tossed her hair back from her face as she came to a swift decision. She would go straight to London. She would phone Ullin from Oban though she wouldn't know what to say. A lump rose into her throat and she caught her lip in her teeth. She loved him, had been quite prepared to live with him in Strathullin House. It was ugly and impractical but at least Claire's influence wasn't in it. A little voice niggled at her. She hadn't been in the house long enough or often enough to know what it was like. It too held memories for Ullin, memories of his first wife. An angry sob shook her. Perhaps she wasn't strong enough or big enough to fight the ghosts of Ullin's past – yet – if he had said he loved her she knew she would have been strong enough for anything.

The vehicle thundered along. Trees, houses, dark hills flew by. Across the black waters of Loch Tuath she saw Ronnach outlined against the sky. Was it real? Had any of it ever been real?

The wind was howling loudly over the moors. The rain that muzzied the windscreen became heavier and she fumbled along the dash panel for the wiper switch. The car swerved and she straightened the wheel too abruptly. She found herself shooting off the road onto a moorland track that was a sea of mud which afforded little grip on the tyres. She fought with the wheel and pressed the brake lever. Rubber squished on mud, there was a jolt that made her teeth rattle, then she felt the car tilting. With a juddering sigh the offside wheels sank into a deep soggy ditch. She threw out a hand to steady herself, there was a soft click and the wipers arched rhythmically across the windscreen. Fooled you, fooled you, they seemed to chant mockingly.

She switched off the engine and the silence of the moors shrouded her. Very carefully she eased herself onto the passenger seat and opened the door. A howling gust of wind tore at it, almost wrenching it from her grasp so that she had to fight to pull it to once more. At least the interior of the car was warm but even so she huddled miserably into her coat, in rising panic listening to the wind shrieking over the vast stretches of empty moorland, battering itself against the car which was shaking alarmingly.

She stared bleakly at the sheet of torrential rain slanting across the windscreen, and feeling a horrific sense of claustrophobia she turned on the ignition. The wipers arched once more and she peered out. The sidelights slanted over the ground in front. The amber marsh grasses were being whipped into a frenzy; a foaming hill burn emphasized the wildness of her surroundings and with a swift movement she cancelled the wipers and sat back.

A great sense of desolation washed over her. What a fool she had been to flee from Stonehurst so impulsively. It might be ages before her absence was discovered. Donald had looked like making a night of it; no one had been around when she had let herself out of the house. She shivered, more from fear than from cold. The car had gone well off the main road and was almost hidden from it by a heathery mound.

She gasped as the car lurched and tilted further into the ditch. If no one came by soon she realized she would have to get out and walk through the black storm-wracked night to Stonehurst which was miles away. Someone was bound to give her a lift, she comforted herself, though it was a small hope. Not one single vehicle had she passed on her flight from Stonehurst and nothing had traversed the road in the last ten minutes.

The seconds of the digital clock on the instrument panel melted away but Chrisann hardly noticed the passing of time, so enmeshed was she in the stream of thoughts that passed in a tangled procession through her mind. She was angry but it was an anger that was turned against herself. She oughtn't to have run off like a spoiled child. She should have stayed and talked everything through with Ullin. He was right. They were partners now, partners for life and that meant giving and sharing. A bitter-sweet longing possessed her. She knew she had to go back, to explain to him her reasons for running away.

She pulled her coat collar closer round her neck and

with a decisive movement opened the door and got out. Immediately the wind seized her and tore at her. Bending herself into it she struggled to keep herself from being blown off the track. The rain swirled round her, blinding her. A roaring filled her ears and she thought that the burn had burst its banks but it came nearer and louder and through the sheets of rain she saw the lights of a large vehicle bobbing along the road. She felt an insane desire to laugh as the Land Rover screeched to a halt and a tall dark figure came running towards her.

"Ullin," she gasped out his name. He reached her and enclosed her fiercely in his arms.

"What the hell are you playing at?" His voice was rough but underlined with such tender concern she found herself clinging to him as she half cried, half laughed with relief.

"Ullin, I'm so sorry," she sobbed. "The car's in a ditch."

"To hell with the car! It's you I came to look for. Donald left ten minutes ago and I discovered you were nowhere in the house so I hopped into the Land Rover and drove like a madman till I saw your lights on the moor."

He was leading her down to the Land Rover and when they reached it he all but lifted her onto the passenger seat before diving round to the driver's door. He revved the engine to drive a short distance to a lay-by where he flicked on the interior light and twisted round to gaze at her, his eyes very blue and intense.

"Ullin, please forgive me," she cried. "I had to get away – to think. I had so much on my mind – and I wasn't sure I liked the idea of living in Stonehurst. The idea of you and Claire in the house – in the bedroom—"

"What gave you that idea?" he asked incredulously. "You've got it all wrong, you darling little fool. The only time I had anything to do with Claire was last year – in Edinburgh. It was just something that happened; I am human and took what she was so ready to give. It was a long time ago – at least it all seems very far off. Since I met you everything else has faded into insignificance. If I had wanted Claire I could have had her *and* Stonehurst but I lost all my reason when you came along. I bought that house for you, Chrisann, and while I'm delighted that I've realized my father's wishes it's your happiness that matters to me. Why did you think I asked you to postpone your London trip? It was to show you the house. I couldn't wait till you came back."

Her heart was singing in her breast and she felt dizzy with wonder. "Oh, Ullin," she murmured. "I *am* an idiot. It was just – Claire said so many things—"

"Claire *has* been a busy little bee," he said bitterly. "She got her venom into you all right but you can forget her now. She left Mull this morning, complete with the proceeds from the sale of Stonehurst. I believe she had a rendezvous with an up and coming Sussex fruit grower she met recently. Trust her to have someone up her sleeve. She won't be lonely for long." His arm came round her waist and he pulled her close to him and pressed his lips against her wet hair. "Don't do this again to me, Chrisann," his voice was husky and filled with tenderness. "You simply must stop running away from me all the time. I love you, my darling, I never thought I'd trust myself to say that to another woman after my wife, but it's true. I've loved you from the moment I saw you serving behind the counter of your father's shop. You were just a skinny teenager but something passed between us that day and I've never forgotten. So, you see, my love for you didn't begin with our meeting on Mull, it goes much further back. I knew all along I'd seen you somewhere before."

"Ullin," she breathed. "You remembered me just as I remembered you. Somehow you were always there – a memory – someone I could never forget. I think I must have loved you for most of my life. And you are right, we are partners now and must share what we have. I'll gladly let you have what you need; money isn't important to me but you are."

"What on earth do you mean?" he asked in amazement, and she saw the pride glinting in his eyes. "I thought I had made it plain to you that *I* am the breadwinner in this partnership. You mistook my meaning back there; I wasn't hinting that you should help me out financially – God forbid I should ever do that! I only meant that there would be occasions when we would have to stay quietly at home and be content with one another. Even successful people have their downs and I'm no exception but Donald brought some mail from Strathullin House and I'm pleased to tell you that I have come up trumps in a property deal worth half a million – so you see, I won't let you starve, my darling. I appreciate your offer though and love you all the more for saying what you did but the wolf is very far from the door I'm glad to say."

She put her slender hand over his strong brown one. "If you don't mind I will be only too happy to stay quietly at home with you as often as possible. I've had enough gadding about to last me for years." She gave a deep sigh of contentment. "I can't wait to have Mum and Dad spend a holiday at Stonehurst and I'm longing to tell Jean – I'm going to miss her."

"Not for long. I'm arranging for them to live in the farmhouse on the estate. Colin Mor will enjoy managing it and Jean will be able to visit Mary when she likes. They're getting on a bit and I know Jean was worried about Jamie getting over to school in the winter. I'll put a younger couple over on Ronnach; I've already got one in mind."

She laughed joyfully. "You really do think of everything, don't you?"

"Not quite, I haven't kissed you this evening." He enfolded her in an embrace that was strong and safe and crushed her mouth in a kiss that was possessive yet filled with such tender love she felt the sting of tears against her lids. Moments stretched, timeless. He held her as if he could never bear to let her go. She felt protected, cherished – and dearly loved. When he finally released her his voice was husky and low. "I'm never letting you go again, my darling, and that's why I've decided to come to London with you. Oh, I know you arranged to stay with a girlfriend but I'm sure she'll understand that a newly married couple ought not to be apart so soon. What do you think?"

"I think," she whispered, "it's the most wonderful idea I've ever heard." She snuggled against him. "Mmm, I feel so good, so complete."

"Not quite." His voice was warm and intimate. "We have some unfinished business to see to – remember?"

She ran her fingers through his hair and murmured. "Yes, I remember and I think I'm going to be very obedient from now on and do as you tell me."

He laughed, a deep happy sound. "If you become too chaste I'll think I'm married to the wrong girl." A frown darkened his brow. "All I want is your trust – and your love."

"You always had my love," she answered seriously, "now you have my trust as well. I'm afraid I've been very very silly but I've learned my lesson and I promise I'll never be influenced again by spiteful insinuations – not now that I know you love me."

He switched on the engine and turned the Land Rover

in the direction of home. The rain had stopped and the clouds were breaking apart. A young moon was riding above the hills of Ronnach; the silvered sea stretched, vast and infinite. It looked like a vision out of a dream but she knew it wasn't a dream any more. It was true and real, just as the big man at her side was real – real and warm and wonderful.

His voice broke into her thoughts. "A new moon, Chrisann, we must make a wish." He pulled up in a lay-by and took her once more into the warm circle of his arms.

"I've already got my wish," she said huskily. "All I could ever want from life." His lips came down on hers and it seemed in those exquisite moments that the sea and the sky held their breath. All around there was silence and peace and love.

Quite a long time later he said rather shakily, "That's one of my wishes fulfilled – now let's go home and make the rest come true. Do you agree?"

"I agree," she breathed obediently and tightened her hold on his waist as they drove homewards through the moon-silvered night.